The Rose Cases: Sylvie's Diary

Circle of Roses, Volume 7

Martha Wickham

Published by Martha Wickham, 2025.

THE ROSE CASES: SYLVIE'S DIARY

First edition. March 31, 2025.

Copyright © 2025 Martha Wickham.

ISBN: 979-8230745204

Written by Martha Wickham.

Table of Contents

"I WANT SYLVIE TO GO to college," Logan said, watching his ex-wife layer mayonnaise onto a sandwich.

"She doesn't seem interested," Lana replied casually.

"Dana's at a big university in Illinois. She started last September and she's happy," Logan said. He glanced up toward the ceiling. "Sylvie!" he called.

"She doesn't have to if she doesn't want to," Lana said, taking a bite of her sandwich.

Sylvie clattered down the stairs, dragging her hand along the banister.

"Do you want to go to college?" Logan asked sharply.

"I don't think so," Sylvie Langly said softly.

"And where would we get the money?" Lana asked, wiping her mouth.

"Government grants," Logan answered. He turned back to Sylvie. "What do you plan to do with your life?"

"I don't know. I guess I'll look for a job soon," Sylvie said, shifting her weight from foot to foot.

"Logan, leave her alone," Lana said.

"Stay out of this," Logan snapped.

"I just graduated last June! I don't even know what I want yet!" Sylvie said, rolling her eyes. I hate arguing with them, she thought bitterly.

Logan scowled and lurched two steps toward her. "You better watch that! I know what's best for you. Too bad your mother doesn't guide you better."

"Give me a break, Dad! What makes you think you can just show up and bark orders?" Sylvie yelled.

Logan's hand rose, deliberate and slow, before slapping her across the face with a heavy thwack.

Sylvie grabbed her purse off the kitchen counter and bolted out the door, her chest tight with anger and hurt.

Lana rushed after her, heart hammering, peering out the door to see where Sylvie had gone.

"She won't get far. She doesn't have much money," Logan said.

"She has some," Lana snapped, grabbing her wallet and keys before bolting out the door.

She jumped into her car but couldn't spot Sylvie anywhere. Maybe she had run the other way.

Hands trembling, Lana whipped the car around and floored the gas pedal.

Still no sign of Sylvie. Heart hammering, Lana raced toward Interstate 65.

She merged onto the freeway, speeding up, scanning the roadside. Panic clawed at her chest.

Realizing Sylvie wasn't there, Lana veered toward an exit—but a blaring horn split the air.

In seconds, two cars slammed into her from different sides, sending her car spinning wildly across the busy freeway.

Metal screamed. Tires shrieked. The world tilted.

Lana's car smashed into a stand of old trees.

The impact crushed the front end—and her legs along with it.

Trapped, blood trickling down her forehead, she gasped once. Darkness closed in.

Lana woke the next day to a blur of light and throbbing pain.

"Mom?" Sylvie's voice broke through the haze.

Lana blinked and stared at the heavy white casts on her legs.

Her stomach growled, and her body screamed for a pain pill.

Sylvie sprinted out. "She's awake!" she called.

A nurse in purple scrubs hurried in, her hair pulled into a bun so tight it looked painful.

"How are we feeling?" she asked, handing Lana a small cup with a pill inside.

"I'm starving," Lana mumbled.

"Of course you are," the nurse said warmly, raising the top half of the bed so Lana could sit up. "I'll get your lunch right away. If you need anything, just press the button." She nodded toward the call button beside the bed.

"Oh, Mom," Sylvie cried, hugging her tightly. "I'll do anything for you. The doctor said if you get a live-in nurse, you can come home this weekend!" Sylvie squealed with excitement.

Lana gingerly touched her head, feeling for wounds.

"You have a concussion and two broken legs," Sylvie explained, her voice soft. "There are some stitches in your left arm from the accident, but don't worry—we'll take care of you. I gave them your insurance card. Dad drove me here. I'm so sorry, Mom. I'll never run out again."

Lana's gaze drifted toward Logan standing outside the room. "I was working on a case for the Circle of Roses. A missing child," she said, her voice trembling. "It's strange—the mother never mentioned the house was haunted. Now she's blaming the ghosts. That child's been missing for about a month... What am I going to tell them?" She shook and took a sip of water.

"You'll be bedridden for a long time, Mom," Sylvie said determinedly. "I'll take over the case. I've been studying how to be psychic—and I'll do their training."

"Okay, if you think you're up for it," Lana said. "I'll call Rose soon. But for now, I need food and rest."

"I'll ask them to give you foods with protein," Logan replied.

"Logan, I'm glad Dana went off to school. She'll be a real lawyer. Nobody could argue like her," Lana added, a hint of pride in her voice.

The nurse brought in a hot plate of chicken soup and rolls with butter. "Eat, you need your strength," she said with a gentle smile.

"We'll leave you alone to eat," Sylvie said. "Is there anything you need?"

"No," Lana answered, shaking her head. The bruise on her face was now fully visible.

With a final wave, they left the room. Once they were gone, Lana breathed a sigh of relief. She began eating, savoring the moment of quiet. I need this silence, she thought.

Lana had decided she wanted to leave the hospital that weekend. A hospital driver drove her home, with her live-in nurse following behind. It was perfect.

Her bedroom was exactly how she had left it, though her daughters had tidied it up. The white bed with its soft blanket and fluffy pillows still filled the room. A large plant sat in the corner, adding coziness, and sunlight poured through the big window. From her bed, she could see straight into the backyard.

Dana and Sylvie were already there.

"Dad dropped me off," Dana said, grinning widely

"What about school?" Lana asked, a hint of concern in her voice.

"I'll only be here today and tomorrow to help. Then I go back to school. It can wait. I don't think I'm going to law school like Dad thought. I'm just taking general classes for now," Dana said, looking uncertain.

"Transfer here," Lana said, excitement in her voice. "You can stay here. I need you, and it won't be some stuffy law school in the city."

"Okay. Let me talk to Dad." Dana ran off to make the call.

"It's perfect, Sylvie. We have a big house, a huge yard, and we're not too far from the college," Lana told her.

"Where will the nurse stay?" Sylvie asked.

"There are two extra rooms," Lana replied.

"He said yes, as long as I promise to visit him. I told him I would. I like Darling, but not that much," Dana said with a playful roll of her eyes.

When the nurse was away, Sylvie and Dana took over the responsibility of caring for their mother. Lana spent most of her time in bed, reading, watching TV, and gazing out the window. Sylvie's first day as a Rose was Monday, but to their surprise, Dana didn't want to join.

"I have school," she told them. "If you need any help, just let me know."

The days were warm and sunny, and Lana longed to sit in the sun. She spent most of her time complaining about her broken legs, which ached deeply. Nurse Ce Ce brought in a wheelchair to help her move around.

On Sylvie's first day as a Rose, she felt nervous, and Dana had to leave for school.

"Just make sure your hair and makeup are done, and speak confidently," her mother advised.

Sylvie wore light brown slacks, a white turtleneck, and a dress jacket. Her dark, layered hair flowed in soft curls. She kissed her mother goodbye before driving off to her first day.

Quietly, she entered the Circle of Roses shop. The hum of activity reminded her of a hair salon, with everyone busy at work.

"Are you Sylvie?" Rose asked, looking up.

"Yes. I'm here to take over my mother's case," Sylvie replied, trying to steady her nerves.

"Okay, I'm Rose, and this is Victoria. We have a file with all the information on your mother's case." Rose led her to a file cabinet and opened it. "I would tell you to grab her notes, but she barely started. All she found out was that a mother living in a haunted house was looking for her missing son." Rose pulled out the case files and handed them to Sylvie. The file contained a picture of the child, his name, and the mother's contact information.

"This place is far—near Darling, Illinois. May I use your phone?" Sylvie asked.

"You can use anything you need," Rose said, gesturing to the phone. She wanted Sylvie to feel welcome. As Sylvie dialed the boy's mother to confirm she'd take the case, Rose slipped into the back room. At her desk, she opened a blue velvet box filled with diamond rose pins that gleamed under the light. She slipped one into her pocket.

Sylvie hung up. "She wants me to meet her there. Afterward, I'll stop by my dad's." Clutching her purse, she added, "I'm heading out now."

Rose nodded. "I have something for you—it means you're officially a Rose." She handed Sylvie a diamond-encrusted rose pin, its facets catching the light in a dazzling sparkle. Sylvie's face lit up with a wide smile. What a surprise—a true welcome to the Circle of Roses.

Sylvie gazed at the glittering diamonds. "Thank you," she said, pinning the rose to her jacket. "See you later," she called, heading out the door.

"Good luck," Rose called after her.

Sylvie faced a nearly two-hour drive. At a gas station stop, she called her father to let him know she'd visit later.

Sylvie arrived, sipping a cherry Coke and studying the house. It was small, weathered, and desperately needed a fresh coat of paint. She knocked on the door.

"Are you here about my missing boy?" the woman asked.

"Yes, I'm Sylvie Langley," she replied.

"Come in. I'm Marge," the woman said. She was heavyset, her dress rumpled, and though she didn't seem depressed, her appearance was disheveled.

"Most of the strange noises come at night," Marge said.

"Have you seen any ghosts?" Sylvie asked.

"Yes, wisps of white smoke drifted from my son's room. Billy complained about them constantly—he's only eight," Marge said.

"Have you contacted the police?" Sylvie asked.

"Yes, I gave them a photo, but they've found nothing. I need a paranormal investigator. Are you experienced?" Marge asked.

"This is my first case, but I've studied paranormal phenomena. I'm with the Circle of Roses," Sylvie said.

Marge eyed Sylvie from head to toe. "Come see his room."

The room looked ordinary at first glance. Sylvie noted the open closet, toys strewn across the floor, and a slightly rumpled bed. "He just vanished from here? Have the ghosts left any traces?" she asked.

"No," Marge said softly.

"May I check the backyard?" Sylvie asked.

Marge nodded, leading Sylvie through the back door. The yard was empty, no clues in sight. "It's strange," Marge said, her voice trembling. "I hear noises like Billy's still in his room—or running. There's a forest across the street, thick with trees. I told him never to go there, but he might have. One day, I came home, and he was gone. His schoolbooks were still on his desk. He didn't always listen, but he did his homework and played with friends. He loved being outside."

"Did the police search the forest?" Sylvie pressed.

"Only briefly," Marge said, frowning.

"I'd like to search it myself. Has his father been told he's missing?" Sylvie asked.

"Yes, but he hasn't seen him. He lives out of town." Marge twisted her dark hair, pinned loosely in a bun.

"I'll explore the forest now and see what I find. I can search more thoroughly tomorrow," Sylvie said.

With Marge's nod, Sylvie crossed the street and stepped into the forest. Shadows cloaked the trees, broken only by faint bird calls and tangled vines. She followed a narrow trail that petered out, an uneasy feeling creeping over her. Near a tree, she spotted scattered garbage. In a clearing, a boy's baby doll lay abandoned. A cold breeze sent a shiver through her. Nearby, a thorny vine clutched a scrap of blue fabric. Heart pounding, Sylvie raced back to the house.

"Look at these," Sylvie said, breathless, showing Marge her finds.

Marge's eyes widened at the doll and fabric scrap. "Those are Billy's! This proves he was in the forest. We need a search team—volunteers, anyone who can help."

"I'll drive through town, show his photo, and ask if anyone's seen him," Sylvie said. "I'll also check with the police for any leads and follow up with you this weekend." A toy truck lay near her feet. Sylvie picked it up, closing her eyes to sense a psychic impression. The same vision flashed as with the doll: a child running through the forest, chasing unfamiliar adults. "Could he have been abducted?" she asked.

"Yes, but I need to know what the ghosts have to do with it," Marge said, her voice strained. "Billy loved the outdoors, but I don't believe he ran away."

"Thank you, Marge. I'll keep you updated," Sylvie said.

Driving away, Sylvie resolved to create missing person posters. She needed to search for answers herself. A stronger psychic vision would help, but her instincts were all she had for now.

Sylvie cruised through the quiet town, its streets nearly empty. Each time she spotted a young boy, she studied his face, searching for Billy's dark hair, brown eyes, chubby cheeks, and the telltale freckle near his ear.

She stopped in a small shop and asked a large man that worked there and made smoothies, if he'd seen him. "His name's Billy." She held up a recent picture.

The man nodded. "A lot of children come in here, but I've seen him more than once. His hair was dirty and his clothes were black. He was with some woman."

"Are you sure?" Sylvie asked.

"Yes, I'd know that frown anywhere," he said.

A lady who worked there wearing a pink dress with brown curly hair said, "I've heard strange things about him."

"From who?" Sylvie asked.

"Just customers. They say he's in a hospital for people who hear voices and that he doesn't have parents. It's a sad case and he was not a happy child." Her name tag read Fiona.

"Do you happen to know what hospital he's in?" Sylvie asked.

"No, sorry," she answered.

"Ok, thank you." Heading towards the door she had a plan. To check every mental hospital in the state. First she went to a store and bought a disposable camera. It was for her investigation and she took pictures of the shop he was seen at. The store she bought it from was just down the road. It was quiet there. You could hear a pin drop in that small town.

She stuffed the camera into her black purse and hit the road to see her father. At that moment, she couldn't wait to see him.

"Sylvie," he called, his voice filled with excitement. She rushed to him, and he hugged her tightly. "What are you up to? Can you stay?" her father, Logan, asked.

"I'm working on that case for Mom. Someone said he's in a mental hospital, so I need to check them. If he's there, why didn't they call his mother?" Sylvie asked, her brow furrowing.

"They probably don't know who the kid is," Logan replied.

"You're right, Dad. You're so right. He's only eight. And I can stay. Actually, I'd like to stay until the case is solved. It's here, not in Chicago," Sylvie said, her voice softening.

"Well, you can stay as long as you want," he said, offering her a reassuring smile. "I'm going to make spaghetti."

"Thanks, Dad!" Sylvie stood up, feeling a surge of gratitude.

"I'll get your things for you," he said, moving toward the door. "I have to go out that way anyway."

The scent of fresh spaghetti filled the air, making Sylvie's stomach growl. "I'll eat first, then get started on the case. I'll check the closest mental hospital."

He nodded in agreement. "I can get your clothes tomorrow." He paused, his gaze lingering on her beautiful rose pin.

"The Circle of Roses gave me this pin. I'm new there," she said, a small smile tugging at her lips. With that, she headed to her room to rest before eating and then investigating the first hospital for Billy.

The second hospital they checked had a dark-haired boy named Billy. It had to be him! The next day, she planned to find out for sure. In the morning, she would go to see him.

When she arrived, Sylvie showed the receptionist a picture.

"Is this boy staying here? His name is Billy."

The receptionist squinted at the photo and checked her computer.

"There's a little boy here by that name. Would you like to see him?"

"Yes, his parents are looking for him," Sylvie said.

The woman stood up to make arrangements for Sylvie to see him right away.

While she waited, Sylvie stepped outside and took a picture of the mental hospital for her records. Inside, patients wandered the halls—some in a daze, others seeming to search for someone. It was heartbreaking. They must not have seen their families often.

A nurse soon came out.

"You can see him now. I'll take you to his room."

They walked up a flight of stairs and stopped in front of a white door with a small window. The nurse left them there. Through the glass, Sylvie noticed deep scratches on the inside of the door—too high and too deep for a boy Billy's size. Maybe a former patient had made them... or something else.

She snapped a quick photo through the window, tucked her camera away, and opened the door.

Billy sat cross-legged on the floor, drawing pictures. When he looked up, Sylvie knew it was him—the same chubby cheeks and small freckle from the photo.

"Hello, Billy," she said gently. "I'm here for your mother. She's looking for you."

He scrambled to his feet.

"My mom? Can I get out of here?" Billy asked eagerly.

"I'm not sure yet," Sylvie said carefully. "Is something wrong with you?"

"Yes, I hear voices," he answered. They are so horrible, he thought.

"That's too bad. Even if you don't go home now, I'll tell your mom you're here and she can come see you. Do they take you out sometimes?" Sylvie asked.

"Yes. We get a smoothie and a fresh cheeseburger. I love them."

"Good, Billy." At least he was alright. His mother would be relieved to hear that.

"Are you seeing ghosts?" she asked.

"Yes, many," he said. "They say things to keep me away from my mother. The people here don't believe me. They think I'm nuts, and they didn't even know where I came from."

Sylvie leaned in, listening carefully.

"One day I was out playing camping. They wouldn't let me back in the house. They told me to wander into the woods and stay there, that my mom was planning to hurt me and didn't want me. Every time I tried to go home, they stopped me and warned me. After a while, I got lost. I passed out and woke up here. They asked me a lot of questions I couldn't answer. They said I was just dehydrated. Whatever." He closed his eyes.

"Your mother does not want to hurt you. I have all your information. I'll give it to the people here, and they can finally call your mother. It must have been a long month for you."

The child stared at the floor, struggling not to cry.

A breeze stirred the air, sudden and cold.

"What?" Sylvie asked.

"A voice told me to run. But I can't go anywhere," Billy said. "I don't want to."

"Let's stop this now," Sylvie said, taking his hand.

Whispering filled the room—sharp, jumbled, and growing louder.

They bolted out of the room and down the stairs.

On the steps, they could hear something chasing close behind.

They sprinted toward the door. Sylvie caught a nurse by the arm and said, "This is a missing child. I'm a psychic investigator hired to find him. I have all his information right here."

She held up papers showing his mother's name and address.

"He needs to be moved immediately. There are ghosts tormenting him, keeping him from his family."

The nurse nodded, quickly grasping the situation. She took the papers and copied the information. Sylvie also snapped a picture of them for her records.

The nurse set about finding a new room for Billy on the first floor, where there were more people around—but no one seemed to be calling his mother.

Sylvie decided to handle it herself.

If all went well, his mother could be here today.

As she had hoped, Billy's mother answered ecstatically: "I'm coming!"

Afterward, Sylvie tried calling her own mother to share the news.

Her mother's nurse answered instead. "She's sleeping," the nurse said.

"Please tell her I found the boy. I'll explain everything when she's feeling better," Sylvie replied.

Next, the police were updated. They said they wanted to speak with Billy.

"He wasn't abducted. He's fine—except for the ghosts he's running from," Sylvie told them.

Finally, she called Rose.

Rose answered, "Okay, it's great he's safe, but the ghosts might still try to find him at home. I'll help you cleanse that house. I'll put together a spell no ghost can withstand. I promise—my intentions will clear it."

"They probably won't travel this far hon. Don't you like being in the roses?" Lana asked.

"No. I think I'll go away to parapsychology school in New York." She got a drink. "I'm serious."

"I know," Lana responded.

Sylvie threw her bags on the chair. "Where's Dana?" she asked loudly.

"I don't know. Probably out shopping," her mom said unsure. She twisted and tried to get comfortable, then took out her pain killers.

Sylvie began looking through her purse hoping the case was over. She took the package of developed pictures.

"They will be so much safer," Lana said.

Sylvie turned on a tall lamp, and looked at the pictures. Billy's info came out mostly clear and the forest looked emerald green. She sat and stared at them. Inside the forest it looked a little smokey. She grabbed a magnifying glass out of the desk. After a while it was clear, some of the smoke formed a being with small eyes. They were the ghosts of the forest. Billy's ghosts.

She looked at the other pictures. There was the same smokey face in the shop window, in the hospital yard's trees, and in the last picture she took of Billy's house that night after they left. They looked like they were watching, waiting for him. She put down the eerie pictures and turned them over.

"They probably won't travel this far, hon. Don't you like being around the roses?" Lana asked.

"No. I think I'll go away to parapsychology school in New York," Sylvie said, grabbing a drink. "I'm serious."

"I know," Lana said quietly.

Sylvie threw her bags onto the chair. "Where's Dana?" she asked, raising her voice.

"I don't know. Probably out shopping," her mom said uncertainly. She shifted, trying to get comfortable, and reached for her painkillers.

Sylvie dug through her purse, hoping the case was finally over. She pulled out the package of developed pictures.

"They'll be much safer now," Lana said.

Sylvie switched on a tall lamp and began flipping through the photos.

Billy's information came out mostly clear, and the forest looked lush and emerald green.

She stared at the images.

Inside the forest, something seemed... smoky.

She grabbed a magnifying glass from the desk drawer.

Looking closer, her heart dropped.

Some of the mist wasn't just smoke—it had formed something.

A being with small, watchful eyes.

The ghosts of the forest. Billy's ghosts.

She turned to the next photo.

There it was again: the same smoky face, peering from the shop window.

In the hospital yard's trees, faint outlines of the same faces.

In the last photo—Billy's house at night—they hovered near the window, watching and waiting.

Sylvie shivered. She flipped the eerie pictures over, face down on the table.

"You have to let the Roses know the case is closed," Lana reminded her.

"I'll call them and tell them. If I decide to go to school, I'll let them know that too. I don't want another case," Sylvie said, her voice firm. "But I'm not quitting. I'll just help when I'm asked."

She stood, gathering herself. "I think I'll go to my room, call Rose, and write in my journal. I want to keep one for all my paranormal experiences. How are you feeling?"

"I'm fine," Lana said. "Just tired and achy. It's hard having broken legs. But my bruises are better, and my headaches have gone away."

"Get some rest," Sylvie said.

She climbed the stairs, passing Dana's bedroom.

Dana was sprawled across her bed, doing homework..

Sylvie flopped onto her bed and opened her new journal.

It was blank.

She needed to make her first entry.

She wrote her name at the top, added the date, and titled the first page: A Rose in the Forest.

Meanwhile, at the Rose Agency, Rose Cortez frowned at her phone.

"We need to hire more people," she said.

"We don't have any other cases right now. You have time," Victoria replied, leaning back in her chair. "But if things are getting this bad, how are you going to keep people? We're not getting paid enough for helping with real cases."

"I know," Rose said, sitting down heavily. "They'll have to do readings, sell merchandise — anything to keep the lights on. Our real job is protecting people from ghosts."

"The harmful kind," Victoria said. "Poltergeists, demons, evil spirits."

Rose nodded grimly and stamped Sylvie's missing boy case CLOSED.

"Maybe we should all go to parapsychology school," she muttered

"I'M INTERESTED IN PARAPSYCHOLOGY. Is there any way we can help out here and learn?" Robin asked. She and her friend Melissa stood in the shop like eager job seekers.

"Yes," Rose said, smiling. "We Roses are looking for people. You'll read, study, and observe in the back. When you're ready, we'll hire you for ghost investigations. They're serious work. Are you both in?"

"Absolutely," Robin said quickly. She glanced at Melissa. "I'm really into ghosts."

"Some of them are bad," Rose warned. "What are your names?"

"Robin and Melissa," Robin answered. Robin had short black hair and a tattoo on her forearm, dressed in black pants. Melissa wore blue jeans and a black T-shirt, her long blond ponytail swinging behind her. "We're roommates."

"I'm Rose, and this is Victoria," Rose said. "Lana and Sylvie aren't here today. Sylvie's heading off to parapsychology school, and Lana's recovering from an accident — she broke her legs."

Rose handed them two books about ghost hunting.

"Do either of you do psychic readings?" she asked.

"No," Robin said with a laugh. "I think those psychics on TV are fake."

"Well, we're the real deal," Rose said, grinning. She motioned for them to sit on a leather couch. "We need help — and you came at the right time. No active cases right now, so it's perfect for training. You'll watch readings, learn the register, and get familiar with equipment for detecting and clearing ghosts."

Robin nodded, and she and Melissa sat down on some floor pillows.

"Go ahead and start reading those books," Rose said. "Watch us work today. Then we'll train you on the register. You can stay a few hours each day until I give you a task to prove you're ready — and strong."

Victoria got up to fetch coffee, and Rose disappeared into the back office.

Melissa leaned toward Robin and whispered, "How long do we have to be in this?"

Robin smirked. "Just until I learn, pass this so-called task, and then make off with what's valuable," she whispered back. "Come on. It'll be fun."

Melissa gave a fake shiver. "Okay... but it's fall — and you know there are real ghosts out there."

"We'll learn how to fight them," Robin said, and they both sat back down on the couch, opening their books to study.

The couch was cozy, and before long they wandered into the mini kitchen, making hot chocolate and chatting about what they were reading. Rose watched them from across the room, pleased they were getting started.

"What do you mean by a task?" Robin asked Rose as she stirred her drink.

"I'll give you a small ghost investigation," Rose explained. "You'll both go together. Even if there are no ghosts, it still counts. It won't involve an actual customer, and I won't make you do fortune-telling unless you want to."

Across the shop, Victoria finished a psychic reading. The customer went up to the register to pay, and the girls watched carefully. The register was an old-fashioned one — no electronics, just a few simple buttons to ring up the total. Rose let them practice with it for a while.

A few more customers trickled in that afternoon, buying incense, rocks, and crystals. Robin and Melissa even tried ringing up some sales themselves. It was a good day's work, and by the end, they were worn out.

"Goodbye, Rose. We're tired," Robin said as they gathered their things. They tucked the ghost-hunting books under their arms, ready to study more at home.

"See you tomorrow," Rose called after them as they disappeared out the door.

Once they got in the car, Robin said, "I wish we didn't live so far away."

"Yeah, but in the end, it'll be worth it," Melissa replied.

Robin sighed as she pulled onto the road. "I feel like I'm abandoning my old job."

Melissa nodded. "There are better jobs out there."

The next day was packed with training. Rose and Victoria taught them everything: how to sell merchandise, how to handle psychic readings, how to keep the shop clean — and most importantly, how to use ghost-hunting tools.

There were detectors that sat on desks, handheld devices that recorded or tracked ghosts, and even apps they could download onto their phones.

Robin didn't like the radar tool. It showed ghost signals — and even though most were just training simulations, the red light flashing across the screen and racing toward her made her jump. A loud, shrieking alarm blared when it happened.

"Don't worry," Rose reassured her. "That's just a training setting. Real ghosts don't usually scream like that."

Still, the sound left Robin rattled. Meeting something that could scream like that wasn't something she ever wanted.

"I want to teach you how to use our video camera next," Rose said. "You'll need it to film your ghost hunt during the task. Later, Victoria and I will review the footage. I'm sending you to an old abandoned school first. If you really find evidence of a haunting, you have to report back to us."

She smiled, proud of their progress. "You've learned the essentials so far. Keep working through your books. You're doing great."

Just then, the vintage bell on the front desk rang sharply. Everyone froze for a moment.

"That bell is supposed to detect ghosts," Victoria said, glancing around.

"It doesn't always mean a ghost is standing right here," Rose added quickly. "But from now on, I'm leaving the bell here permanently. I'll secure it to the desk, so if anything comes into the shop, we'll know immediately."

The bell sat in the right-hand corner of the room near the windows, quietly swinging on its own for a moment before going still.

As Robin and Melissa checked out their equipment and gathered their books, Rose joked, "We ought to start our own parapsychology school."

Everyone laughed, but a quiet tension still lingered in the air.

"What do you think of learning ghost hunting?" Robin asked, standing on the curb outside their large mansion, where she and Melissa lived with a few others.

"It's fine. I'm not that into it," Melissa replied, tugging at her jacket as the cold wind blew. "When it's over, I want to go to a regular school. I like my life here at the mansion, too."

Robin shrugged, flicking her cigarette into the dirt. "I like it. If I get one of those gnarly ghost detectors, I want to use it here in the mansion. They have this ghost box. And Halloween's in a few weeks." She paused, eyes glinting with mischief. "I could try to swipe one from the redhead."

"Maybe we can ask her to buy us one, and we'll use our pay," Melissa suggested, but her voice dropped as she glanced at the shop's bell ringing faintly in the breeze. "But I don't like that bell. When it goes off, it's not a good sign. And sometimes, you can't even see the ghosts. Even if they're harmless, it's still creepy."

The wind howled again, pulling at their hair. "I'm going inside," Melissa said, shivering slightly.

"Just remember, we've got to go back to Rose's crystal shop later today," Robin reminded her, looking out toward the distant mountains. Their mansion sat isolated in the middle of nowhere. The wind made it feel even more remote. "We'll learn about the occult for a bit more."

Melissa nodded, but the chill in the air made her want to retreat inside.

Rose, meanwhile, was on her way to the abandoned school, a place she'd sent the two trainees to that evening. The school was run down, a place on the verge of collapse, but it could still be entered. It would be an ideal place to test their skills, though the atmosphere was anything but ideal. The wind howled through the building, making eerie noises, and the air felt heavy with an unsettling energy.

Rose had planned to set the location up to appear haunted, but as she arrived, she quickly realized it would be impossible to fake. Even if the school wasn't haunted, the girls would likely sense something. They had to face the challenge of the unknown.

She felt a familiar sense of dread settle over her as she stepped closer to the building. It was the same feeling she'd had when she feared losing her shop—a tightness in her chest, a sense of vulnerability. She shook it off. There was no use dwelling on it now. As long as people kept coming to the shop, they were fine.

She made the sign of the cross as she walked back to her car, hoping the trainees would have a successful night. She planned to return around nine, but she trusted the girls would be safe. After all, it was just a ghost hunt—what could go wrong?

Robin led the way through the school's main entrance, with Melissa trailing behind her. Robin's backpack weighed heavily on her shoulders, filled with the ghost-hunting gear they'd been given. The ghost box, camera, and flashlight were packed carefully inside. It was getting late—just two hours until the sun would set—and they needed to be prepared.

She passed the camera to Melissa and stepped in front of it, ready to film. This could be easier than she thought.

"We're inside the school," Robin said, pointing toward the hallway. The floor was cluttered with broken branches, discarded papers, boxes, and old wooden desks left to rot. "This place was built over seventy years ago, an elementary school. And, from what I've heard, it's rumored to be haunted."

She turned on the ghost box, the plastic device humming softly as its buttons lit up. It was simple but functional, the kind of equipment you only needed if you were serious about ghost hunting.

With the flashlight tucked into her pocket, Robin led the way to the first classroom. Their footsteps crunched on the debris, and the wind moaned through the cracked windows. The place felt like it was holding its breath.

They moved to the next room, and Robin's nose wrinkled. The air was stale, and the room was a wreck—walls covered in random scribbles and old furniture scattered about.

For a moment, they just stood there, taking in the scene. "Can you imagine how many kids learned in a place like this?" Robin mused quietly. Then, without another word, they moved on to the next classroom.

The desks in this room were equally destroyed, but there was something unsettling about them. The surface of one desk was scrawled with a name: Sherry was here. Robin bent down, her fingers hovering near the worn wood.

"Come here," Robin called to Melissa, her voice tight.

When Melissa approached, she leaned in to read what was now written: Help me.

"Do you think the teachers were mean?" Melissa asked, her voice laced with uncertainty, eyes wide as she scanned the room.

Robin shook her head, a chill creeping up her spine. "No... I'm betting a ghost wrote that."

Suddenly, a low moan echoed from somewhere deeper in the building. The sound vibrated through the walls. Robin's heart raced as she grabbed the camera from Melissa's hands.

"Record that," she said sharply. "And let's get out of here."

"I got it." Melissa turned on the camera as they made their way quickly toward the door.

"Wait!" Robin froze for a second, looking down at her ghost box. The light was flashing red. She felt a cold shiver run through her. "We have to prove it was a real ghost."

Melissa kept the camera running as they backed toward the door. The distant sound of heavy footsteps rang through the hall, growing louder.

"Don't stop recording," Robin urged. "Let's go. Now."

They burst out the door, the camera still filming as they ran down the steps and toward the car. Robin fumbled with the keys, her hands shaking, as she started the engine.

As they sped away, the school faded behind them, but something didn't sit right. The entry door creaked open, just a little, as if something—or someone—was watching them leave. Robin pushed harder on the gas.

"I want to go home," Melissa whispered, her voice tense.

"We're going to Rose's shop, The Circle of Roses," Robin said, her gaze fixed straight ahead. "We'll show them the video and the ghost box. They'll know it's haunted. And there's nothing anyone can do about it. I'm not coming back."

Melissa slouched in her seat, her face pale as the sun dipped lower, leaving only a faint orange glow on the horizon.

"Robin..." Melissa's voice was barely a whisper. "I think it's following us."

Robin glanced in the rear-view mirror, her heart pounding as she saw the green orb still trailing behind them. It was almost as if it was chasing them. She gripped the steering wheel tighter.

"This thing won't follow us to the shop," Robin muttered under her breath. "If it does, I'm not getting out of the car." She slammed her foot on the gas, speeding toward the shop. But the orb matched her pace, moving faster with every mile.

When she finally screeched to a halt outside the shop, the car skidded—about four feet, the tires screeching against the pavement. Victoria and Rose came rushing out.

"Whoa," Rose called, stepping back in surprise.

"Safe!" Robin shouted, her voice a mix of relief and defiance. "The school is haunted. We got it on tape. I had to speed all the way here because it was following us." She tossed the camera to Rose with a quick nod.

They started heading inside, the night air cool and sharp against their skin. Robin's mind raced. We're not safe from that thing yet.

"This means you're roses now," Rose said, a lightness in her voice as she gave them an approving look.

Melissa, walking a step behind, let out a quiet sigh. I wonder when we're going to steal and run, she thought to herself. I'll ask later.

The sound of loud clapping echoed behind them, and Robin grinned, feeling the strange weight of the situation lighten just a little.

"We have a job now," Robin announced, excitement creeping into her voice.

"You'll get paid every Friday," Rose said, nodding with satisfaction.

"Awesome," Robin said, slumping into a chair as they sat down with soda and cookies. Rose gestured for Robin to follow her.

As Rose gave Robin a tour of the shop, Melissa couldn't shake the feeling that something was off. Her eyes kept darting to the windows, scanning for any sign of the ghostly orb. But there was nothing. The space around them felt heavy, quiet.

She wandered over to the room with the old ghost bell—the one Rose had left on the desk. Everything was still. Too still, Melissa thought.

She sat down in the corner, her thoughts racing. Maybe this business wasn't so bad. Maybe I don't need to steal and run after all. But as the sky darkened, she felt the exhaustion of the long day creep in, mingling with her unease.

Rose's voice broke through her thoughts. "Be here tomorrow morning," she called, signaling the end of the day.

Melissa stood up slowly, still glancing toward the windows. She poked her head out the door, looking for any sign of the orb.

"Is he there?" Rose asked with a teasing smile.

Melissa shook her head, a relieved breath escaping her lips as she took her ponytail out and let her hair fall loose.

"No," she said softly. But something still gnawed at her.

They headed toward the car without incident. Robin started the engine, glancing at Melissa with a knowing look.

"Go. I don't want it to follow us," Melissa said, her voice tight.

Robin didn't need any more convincing. She pressed her foot on the pedal, and they sped away from the shop, leaving the strange and unnerving night behind them.

When they finally reached the country mansion, they went straight to their rooms. Melissa collapsed onto her bed with a sigh, her mind still spinning.

"I don't want to go tomorrow," she admitted, her voice barely above a whisper. The thought of facing whatever might come next felt overwhelming.

Robin snapped her fingers. "Don't worry. I saw where Rose keeps a box of diamond rose pins. Must be worth thousands. There were so many, and when they're not around, I'll go to the register and get the money. We'll have it all, and we can stay out here as long as we want."

Melissa, barely paying attention, nodded, her eyes glued to an old movie playing on the TV. Robin smiled to herself, already plotting her next move as she danced toward the closet to stash her backpack.

After dinner, the house settled into an eerie quiet. But as they lay in bed, the sounds of creaking floorboards filled the air. Melissa stiffened, her eyes darting around the room.

"That's nothing," Robin said, her voice casual. "There's going to be all kinds of noises in this huge country house. I'm sure that ghost can't find us."

Melissa turned her head, squeezing her eyes shut. She told herself to ignore the sounds, but something about the night felt off.

Meanwhile, Robin could hear footsteps echoing down the hall, the soft murmur of voices drifting through the walls. It was a long night.

Sylvie sat alone at the shop, her sweater snug against the crisp fall air. She glanced out the window, noting Robin standing just outside, her eyes fixed on the store. It made Sylvie uneasy.

Inside, a woman purchased a large rose quartz crystal for her collection. Sylvie absentmindedly played with some small fool's gold rocks on the counter, her mind elsewhere. What is she doing? Sylvie wondered, but it was none of her business. She'd taken a break from the roses after finishing the missing boy case, and had been doing her best to keep a low profile since.

The phone rang, breaking her thoughts. A customer wanted to schedule a reading, and though the shop had been getting more bookings with Halloween approaching, Sylvie still felt the weight of something unsettling. They didn't even have a medium to speak to the dead, but the business was picking up. Robin standing outside the shop was strange, but not so much as to raise alarms.

As the day stretched on, Sylvie decided to take a quick break. She stood and made her way to the restroom, splashing cold water on her face. The sound of a small bang echoed through the store, followed by the faint jingle of the bell above the door.

What was that? Sylvie's heart skipped a beat.

She rushed to the store entrance. Her stomach dropped.

The shop was in chaos. Some of the crystals were gone, and the desk drawers had been pulled out and scattered across the floor. Robin's presence had disappeared. Sylvie's mind raced as she ran to the desk. The gold pens were missing. The box filled with diamond pins was gone too.

Panic began to rise. Sylvie checked the register—empty. She stumbled outside, frantically scanning the area for any sign of Robin. A few shoppers milled around the strip mall, unaware of the crime that had just taken place.

Sylvie pulled out her phone, her hands shaking as she dialed the police. She'd barely hung up when she called her mom. "I don't know what happened. The shop's been robbed," she explained, her voice a mix of confusion and fear.

Moments later, the sirens wailed in the distance, growing louder as the police pulled up. Rose arrived at the door, breathless, her eyes wide with concern.

"What happened?" Rose asked, her voice thick with worry.

Sylvie stood, her face pale and tear-streaked. "We were robbed. I came to clean, and I saw this short, dark-haired lady staring at me and the shop. I went to the bathroom, and then I heard a noise. The desk drawers—they fell to the floor. Crystals, pens, pins... and the money's gone. This is awful." Her voice cracked as she wiped her eyes. "I shouldn't have gone to the bathroom. I called the cops... and my mom."

Robin and Melissa. Sylvie's mind raced.

Rose stepped forward, her voice calm but firm. "Don't cry, Sylvie. I know who did it. Robin and Melissa," she told the officers as they entered. "But I don't know much about them. The circle of roses... it's over. I can feel it."

The cops nodded, beginning to take fingerprints. "We'll find them," one assured her.

"Thank you," Rose said, her voice steady despite the situation. "I'm Rose. This is my shop. They didn't come in today." She turned to leave and headed to her mini-lab, closing the door behind her. She pulled out her crystal ball, lit a candle, and whispered, "Where does Robin the rose live?"

The smoke swirled, and suddenly both girls appeared in a yard—beyond it, a dark mansion loomed. The windows flickered with dim light. Rose's stomach sank when she saw a pentagram etched into the glass and a cauldron sitting by the window. Occult, she realized. They had completely fooled me.

She needed answers.

Rose turned to Sylvie. "Are there any occultists in Darling, Illinois?"

Sylvie thought for a moment. "I know of one... They live in a big, dark house about twenty miles from the graveyard. My dad may know of more."

"Why?" Sylvie added, her voice tinged with curiosity. "Do you think the thieves are involved with the occult?"

"Yes. Come with me," Rose insisted, her resolve hardening.

They both headed to the mini-lab. Sylvie's eyes widened at the sight: a glass tube filled with green liquid, shelves lined with mysterious jars, and an unused cauldron resting on the counter.

"This is my lab," Rose said with a wry smile.

How cool is this? Sylvie thought, impressed by the hidden space. I'm in.

Rose lit the candle again. The mansion reappeared in the smoke. "Is this the occult's house in Darling?" she asked, her gaze fixed on Sylvie.

"Yes," Sylvie replied. "In high school, we all stayed away from it."

Rose's expression was set. "Take me there."

They grabbed their purses and headed to Rose's van. Sylvie directed her as they drove.

It was a long drive, and by the time they arrived, Sylvie needed to call both of her parents. They'd be spending the night at Sylvie's dad's house, and the next day, they would go to the mansion.

Night had fallen by the time they reached Sylvie's father's place. The house was quiet—two empty bedrooms, since Dana was gone. It was perfect. They quietly made their way to their rooms, knowing that tomorrow would bring them closer to the strange mansion.

The mansion was easy to find, but getting inside wouldn't be. People wandered around outside, and anyone could be skilled in witchcraft. They parked a little distance away, careful not to draw attention. Rose approached a young woman standing near the entrance. "Do you know a blonde girl named Melissa who lives here?" she asked.

The woman pointed to the left, her finger tracing the outline of a black cape. What is she studying in the occult? Rose wondered.

When Rose saw Melissa hanging by the trees, she gave Sylvie a thumbs up and moved quickly toward her.

As she neared, she saw the rose pin sparkling against Melissa's sweater. "Melissa! Why do you live here? Are you into witchcraft?" Rose called out.

"No, Robin is," Melissa answered. "I'm into ghosts and demons."

Rose reached out. "Give me that pin. It belongs to the roses," she demanded, tugging at the pin on Melissa's sweater. It tore, but didn't come off. "I want everything back. Where's Robin?"

"I don't know!" Melissa shouted, her voice high and strained. People around them started to stare, which made Rose uneasy.

Rose turned and quickly returned to the car. She called the police. "They'll be here soon," she said, then motioned for Sylvie to stay in the car while she ran inside the mansion to speak to someone in charge.

Passing a large library near the entrance, Rose found a man seated at a desk, wearing a dark robe that resembled a monk's habit. "Robin and Melissa stole from me. Where do they stay?" she asked, her tone firm.

The man raised an eyebrow, his gaze skeptical. "Those are serious accusations. Are you a student here?"

"No," Rose replied, already stepping past him. She ran up the stairs, determined to find Robin. Looking out the back window, she could see where the girls had their classes.

The man followed her, blocking the door. "Where do they stay?" Rose demanded, frustration creeping into her voice

"I won't tell you until you tell me who you are," he said, his tone cold and dismissive.

Rose was surprised when Melissa approached them slowly, almost cautiously, instead of running. "This is Rose. Robin and I work at her psychic shop," she said, her voice soft.

"I'm sorry," Rose apologized, feeling a bit guilty for confronting Melissa and tearing the pin from her sweater. "Robin robbed my shop, and you're wearing the pin."

"It's beautiful," Melissa said, her eyes softening as she looked at the pin. "Come on, I'll take you to my room." She led them upstairs, and Rose followed with Sylvie close behind.

When they reached the room, a man with an air of authority stood by the door, watching them. "Is it true?" he asked.

"Yes," Melissa replied, her voice steady. "Robin stole everything. We have the pins, the pens, and the money." She turned to Rose. "This is Edgar. The owner and leader of the occult practices here. He's pagan, but harmless."

"Why didn't you tell me Robin was doing this?" Edgar's voice had a note of frustration.

"I couldn't," Melissa answered quietly.

"Melissa, give me the pins and the money. It'll be okay." Rose turned to Edgar. "I'm not sure where the money is, but I know where the pins are." She pulled the white box from Melissa's hands and began to take out the pins. Melissa, without protest, started to remove the one she was wearing.

"No," Rose stopped her. "You keep that one. For your honesty. And if you want to keep working at my shop, you can."

Just as they were speaking, the sound of footsteps approaching the stairs made them turn. Robin appeared in the doorway, looking confused. "What's going on here?" she asked, eyes darting from one face to the next.

"She knows you stole everything," Melissa said coldly.

The sudden sound of sirens echoed outside, and without a second thought, Robin bolted for the door. The officers, who had arrived just in time, chased after her. They caught her before she could make it out.

As they slapped the handcuffs on her, one officer turned to Melissa. "Is this the thief?"

"Yes, officer," Melissa replied, her voice steady but emotionless.

As Robin was dragged away, she managed to reach into her pocket and pull out a small magic wand. Though her hands were cuffed in front of her, she raised it and pointed it directly at Rose. "May your business fail," she muttered, her voice laced with venom. "The elements will prevail. So seals this curse."

The officers didn't react, too focused on getting Robin into the car, but Rose, Sylvie, and Melissa exchanged looks, unsure of the curse's meaning.

"I hope she stays in jail for a long time," Rose said, shaking her head.

She turned to Melissa. "Will you be coming back to work for me?"

Melissa considered it for a moment. "Sure, why not? I'd have to move closer, though. There should be a mansion I could stay in out there," she added with a hint of humor.

Rose nodded, a small smile playing on her lips.

"Are you sure? You could both take classes here," Edgar said, his tone curious but respectful.

"I like it out here, but I'd prefer to stay in my new job," Melissa explained, clearly tired of the whole school experience.

Edgar gave a nod of respect. "Fair enough."

"We're heading back to Sylvie's house now. After that, I'll need to call the shop. This time, I need your full name, address, and phone number," Rose said, her tone businesslike.

"Sure thing. I'll be there bright and early Monday morning," Melissa replied, sounding a bit more confident now. With that, they headed out, and Melissa began to think about moving to a school closer to central Chicago.

As they got in the car, Rose glanced over at Sylvie. "Robin was arrested, and I'm keeping Melissa. It was only Robin who stole." She raised her fists in excitement. "I need to call the shop when we get to your dad's. Robin was mumbling some mumbo jumbo about the business," she said, her voice mixed with frustration and determination. She started the car, and they drove off. Sylvie felt a wave of relief.

In the shop, Victoria was lighting the small stove in the kitchen to boil some water. "I heard you were at parapsychology school," she asked Sylvie.

"I haven't started yet. So far, it hasn't been easy being a Rose, but I want to be here," Sylvie responded.

"And it stays here," Victoria said with a smile. "We've got an assignment coming up— a haunted asylum."

"How exciting!" Sylvie said, laughing. "If I can get a paycheck here, I can study in this town like Dana. I can't stand her, but it's okay."

Suddenly, the old vintage bell in the classroom went off. "What was that?" Sylvie asked, looking up in surprise.

"It's the ghost alarm. Remember? Rose set it up during the meeting," Victoria said, her voice a bit more serious. They quickly ran toward the sound.

When they reached the room, there was nothing there. "Hello?" Victoria called out, her voice echoing. She grabbed the ghost box from a desk and turned it on. The light flashed green, signaling the presence of a ghost. "Fern was around here. I haven't seen her though," she said, frowning.

"Maybe that's her," Sylvie said, feeling uneasy

Victoria walked around the room, ghost box in hand. They heard shuffling noises, then silence. Suddenly, the sharp scent of smoke filled the air, and they both turned toward the main shop. The fire was coming from the small kitchen! The stove, which Victoria had lit earlier, had caught a picture on the wall, and the flames were spreading fast.

Without thinking, they grabbed a large blanket and smothered the fire, then Victoria grabbed the pan and threw it into the oven. "How did that happen?" she muttered, looking at the small part of the wall that had burned black.

Sylvie opened a window to let out the smoke just as the phone rang. It was Rose, sounding worried. She quickly relayed the news about Robin's arrest and Melissa's new status as a Rose, but she was still concerned since Robin had tried to curse the shop.

"We just had a small fire," Victoria said, trying to keep calm.

"I'll be back tomorrow. I want to see how much damage Robin's curse has done," Rose said.

"Alright, yes, please come back. How are you?" Victoria asked.

"I'm alright, just worried about you guys over there," Rose replied, her voice still tinged with concern.

"If Robin's in jail, she can't cast spells on the store. They probably confiscated her wand," Victoria said, trying to reassure Rose.

"Good thinking, Victoria," Rose said. "Should I make you my assistant, maybe an assistant manager? You've been here since the beginning."

Victoria smiled slightly. "We'll see," she said before hanging up the phone.

"That was Rose. She thinks this place has been cursed," Victoria said, glancing at Sylvie.

"You never know. I thought it was the ghost," Sylvie said, her voice wavering slightly.

"Who knows," Victoria muttered. "I'd hate to see this place go up in smoke." They spent some time looking for the ghost that had set off the bell. No one was in the kitchen, and the ghost box didn't detect any ghosts there.

Asylum Stop

Rose

I HAD NEVER BEEN CALLED a fake before, but someone decided to trash our shop window by throwing eggs and writing "fake" on the glass. When we saw it, Victoria and I immediately started cleaning it off. Sylvie, who wasn't as tall as me and Victoria, came over to help as soon as she saw what had happened. I'm glad she's here.

What this tells me is that people in the community don't believe in us. But I, Rose Cortez, am determined to build a more trusting reputation. "Don't worry, Sylvie. I'll show them we're real," I told her as we wiped down the windows. "I'll prove it when we investigate Blackwood Asylum. Strange sounds and occurrences have been reported there— it was like a torture chamber. I'll bring a recorder, and if you bring one too, it'll help. We can split up and capture video footage from two different angles of that huge asylum. Okay?"

"Yes," Sylvie replied. "I'm thinking of keeping a diary of all my investigations, so I'll make notes in the recordings. What if we get split up?"

"We'll find a place to meet up," I reassured her. "Victoria is coming too, and we'll go in the day." She seemed satisfied with that. Her dark hair and soft complexion gave her a grounded, approachable vibe.

"I wonder if we can prove there's life after death and make a lot of money?" Victoria mused.

We all laughed. "We can try, but I think that's just sensationalism," I said. Victoria smiled. "We could split it," I added, sugarcoating the odds. I mean, if there are so many books and pictures about ghosts, hasn't somebody already proven it? Or maybe it's just a contest.

"What about the pictures Sylvie took?" I asked, remembering. She had said the missing boy investigation revealed the same evil ghost in some of the photos she had taken around there. The asylum investigation is tomorrow— it'll be like a field trip.

I pulled out my video camera when we reached Blackwood. The place was a mess—an abandoned scene with little left behind. Trash littered the ground, and I almost tripped as I walked through it. I turned on my camera and set it down on a desk. "We'll split up, and in an hour, we'll meet back here by the entrance," I said.

It was perfect—cloudy and cool, with jackets on as I could see rain clouds gathering outside. The van was parked as close to the building as possible. All three of us separated: I went right, Victoria headed upstairs, and Sylvie went left toward the basement. I'd never seen so much decay before.

Sylvie

"This is Sylvia Olivia Langly," I said into the camera, my voice steady. "We're about to begin our investigation of Blackwood Asylum. This is my video diary of tonight's events, and from the looks of things, I believe this place is haunted."

I looked around, and when I saw a door, I called out, "What is this?" I tugged on the door, which opened into pitch-blackness, warm air flooding out. The stairs went straight down. I switched on the flashlight taped to the recorder and descended. The basement. I shivered at the thought of what might have happened down there. I left the door open for light and air.

"I found the basement!" I called, not sure if anyone could hear me. As I made my way down the stairs, I heard mice scurrying and the building creaking. I wandered around, feeling uneasy but determined to stay. The noises were hard to place—could be mice, could be me, could be a ghost.

The basement stretched into darkness with a long tunnel. I stopped before venturing in. Behind me, old beds with straps sat in the gloom. I pushed forward. I took a deep breath. The point of this investigation was to gain experience and prove that ghosts exist—that psychics like me are real.

As I walked deeper into the tunnel, I thought I heard breathing that wasn't mine. It wasn't. My heart raced, and then I heard footsteps behind me. I whipped around but saw nothing. Panic surged through me as I started running down the tunnel, not knowing where it would lead. I found the first room I could, slammed the door, and locked it.

The knob began to turn. I backed up and screamed, "Rose!" as loud as I could.

No one came. The thing on the other side of the door couldn't get in. I heard echoes, distant voices, but they weren't Rose or Victoria. The voices were... men. My mind raced. The tunnel seemed endless. And then—there it was again. I ran out of that basement as fast as I could! Rose and Victoria joined me and it took seconds to get to the car. As I got in, Rose took a picture of what was chasing me. She took a few of them.

Victoria

That night, I opened the backdoor for some fresh air. Even I was uneasy about what might be lurking outside after everything that happened that day. I'm brave, but not that brave. We were Roses, ghost hunters, and the ghosts knew that. I dumped out the trash and quickly went back inside.

The screams from the asylum kept echoing in my mind. When the phone rang, I jumped. It was Rose! "Hi! It's going to take a while to make the commercial, so I'm just going over the footage. I've also filmed some readings and the front of the store. It'll be great. I'll send everything off to a professional company for editing, and it should bring in more business. I'm going to send the footage with an essay to that wealthy man, explaining everything that happened and how we're the ones who can prove there's life after death. We're paranormal investigators. If we get a lot of money from this, it'll help the business, and I'll make sure you and Sylvie get bonuses. Maybe we can even move to a bigger, busier location. How does that sound?" she asked.

"Great," I replied. "If I can help with anything, just let me know." The money sounded good, but were those contests to prove there's life after death even real? I didn't want to question it out loud.

Rose sent in the essay right away, and when I saw the commercial, it was incredible. Her home video camera made everything look so authentic. When the commercial aired, it boosted our business, especially on weekends. Rose and I worked tirelessly, but Sylvie wasn't exactly connecting with customers through readings. She was more focused on selling products.

As a customer was leaving, she turned to Rose and said, "Thank you. After the last reading, I found my lost dog."

Rose smiled. "You're welcome." She then picked up an envelope she had received in the mail. It was from the essay contest to prove there's an afterlife. She glanced at me, opened it slowly, and held her breath as she read.

Her eyes widened, and she flipped to the second page. She turned it toward me. There was a check for two hundred thousand dollars! She gasped, "They said they were impressed by our commercial! All our money problems are solved. I want to move."

I stared at the check, unsure if it was real, but Rose didn't hesitate. She went straight to the bank and deposited it. It was the greatest thing that had happened to us. All that good energy Rose had put out was finally coming back to us. I knew what the next few days would entail: cleaning, packing, and searching for a fancier, new shop.

Our new paychecks came with a thousand-dollar bonus. That commercial had really paid off. Rose wanted to use the extra money to buy a building for the store, not just pay rent. As she started looking at larger spaces, I told her, "You're going to need a lot of products to fill a bigger store."

"That's okay," she replied. "I won't go too big, but people will definitely notice a bigger store." She was right. The last place was tucked in a strip mall by a busy road, surrounded by other shops. I could tell her dream had finally come true. She had proven herself, won the money, and wasn't about to lose her shop. She was unstoppable.

As we prepared to move into a bigger, nicer building, the ghost detector bell remained silent, so we had to bring it with us to the new shop. Standing in the doorway of the old Roses Crystal shop, I tried to take it all in. The beginning—Frankenstein's bride, the zombies, and the thieves who tried to destroy everything we had built. It had all started as Sylvie's and my only jobs, and now we were moving forward. Soon, the old shop would just be a memory.

Looking at the new place, I knew we were about to make something even better. We would have the shop, a reading room for psychics, and a training room for paranormal investigation. And, of course, a break room and a bathroom. My guess is that the last business that occupied the space had been respectable, with receptionists and everything. It just had that vibe. I couldn't wait to get started, and I knew the other two girls felt the same way. This was only the beginning.

A ROSE'S WORK IS NEVER done. "We're real, and I've proved it, but I want to know if the Bride of Frankenstein was real," Rose said to Sylvie.

"Where would you start?" Sylvie asked.

"All I know is, if I knew where she had family, I could learn more about the bride. Her name was Terra. My guess is she wasn't the original Bride of Frankenstein, but she came back from the dead and looked like her. Most people don't believe in zombies, but I do. Her boyfriends were zombies too. She's the original enemy of the roses, Sylvie."

Sylvie nodded. "I wonder if she has a family tree. Let's look and see," she said.

The family tree traced from Therese to Terra, to Tyra, to Louise, to Justine Anderson. There was a contact button for those with an account. Sylvie and Rose high-fived each other, and Rose paused to think about what to say in the email. She didn't want to make this woman an enemy, even though she had killed her mother when she was a zombie. Finally, she began typing.

Email to Justine:

Justine,

I'm writing with great interest after seeing your family tree. I noticed that you are related to Terra Belinda Green. You might have heard that she's been called the Bride of Frankenstein. With that knowledge, I'd like to ask you a few questions, if that's okay. I'm a psychic shop owner from Chicago, so please let me know if we can talk. Thank you so much.

Rose

The response came quickly.

Reply from Justine:

Rose,

Yes, I've heard of the Bride of Frankenstein. I don't believe it, but she did seem like it. I'm her great-granddaughter, Justine Anderson. I live alone in a large one-story house at the end of a street. It's lonely, and the house is haunted. People have tried to visit, but the house gets deathly still, and they leave. If you want to talk, feel free to reach out. Do you hunt for ghosts? If so, would you be willing to meet me at my house? Let me know, and I'll send you my contact information. I think this meeting could help with the house's negative impact on me.

Justine

Rose's Reply:

Justine,

I'd love to meet and assess the situation. I'm more than willing to help in any way possible. Could you send me your phone number and address? I'll also provide my contact information. Looking forward to hearing from you.

Everything was set. Rose knew that this woman wouldn't be an enemy. She had seen it before—some nasty ghost runs everyone out, but the owner remains, lonely and trapped by the spirit. Those people never wanted the presence in their house. But there was one thing—Rose didn't want the other girls in the circle of roses to know about Justine. Because Justine was Terra's great-granddaughter, the others might be afraid. They'd worry that Terra's ghost would come back to haunt them, or that the problem was too big for them to handle. They could have freaked out the moment they saw Justine's face. So, Justine and her case were a secret—for now.

When Rose and Justine met at her house, it was quiet—eerily so. Justine was the only one there. From what Rose had heard, her husband had left a long time ago. They'd argued endlessly, couldn't agree on anything, and eventually, boredom took its toll. He left and quickly found someone else. After that, everything spiraled downward.

"The ghosts are a jinx," Justine said. "One of them scared my dog by turning on all the appliances. It was so loud he bolted out the doggy door, dug a hole, and ran toward the road. He was found dead a week later, hit by a big truck. My poor Brandon. He was so sweet. No one saw it coming."

Justine's long, straight hair hung lifeless, and her pale skin only accentuated the darkness in her eyes—nearly black. She was a woman weighed down by sadness, each word she spoke heavy with grief.

"Do you know if anyone died in this house?" Rose asked gently.

"No, not that I know of. You'd think someone had, though. I see ghosts who look like murder victims. And I've seen my family. A dead bride with a gray streak in her hair. Ghosts held together by threads. My grandma Tyra, who died about fifteen years ago. She used to watch over me and make noise. I believe they're still here. Terra wasn't the Bride of Frankenstein. She didn't like him. She liked Nathaniel Johnston. He was perfect for her. I wish these ghosts could go somewhere else," Justine explained, her voice trembling slightly.

"Do you know why Terra was a zombie?" Rose asked.

Justine nodded slowly. "So someone could bring her back and have a girlfriend. She wasn't alive, but dead. She wanted another dead person," she said with a sad smile. "All that Frankenstein stuff was just legend. But I believe in zombies."

"Me too," Rose agreed quietly.

Justine poured them both tea. "I have a brother named Jon who lives in Michigan. My mother's name is Louise."

"That's a nice name," Rose said, taking a sip.

"My grandparents were Tyra and Gary. They were good people. My grandma was happy when she wasn't talking about ghosts. She didn't like the old house they lived in—it was called The Shadows. There was a replica built, but I've never seen it." Justine paused, her eyes flicking toward the ceiling. "That was a ghost." The distinct sound of bangs echoed above them, like someone was up there.

Rose's eyes scanned the room. "Is there anything the ghosts have done that I could see?"

"No, but I don't like it here. If I move, they may follow me." Justine stared at the corner. "I see a shadow ghost there. It has a rope around its neck."

Rose caught a glimpse of it for a second before it vanished. "We definitely need to do some work here," she said, determination creeping into her voice. "I have an idea."

Justine watched her, waiting. "These ghosts are very attached to this place," Rose continued. "There are herbs that can protect you from evil spirits. Different herbs for different purposes. Spanish moss and scotch broom are two, but fennel is the best. You can drink it like tea, and the ghosts will probably go. There's also a golden chalice that's blessed—if I can get it for you."

"Really? Oh, thank you, Rose. It's so gloomy here, but I don't want to leave. What are the odds it will work?" Justine asked, hope creeping into her voice.

"There's a ninety-five percent chance it will work, and it's good for you," Rose said.

"Count me in! I'll go to Germany if I have to. You know, me and my ex had this lovely wedding planned, but we couldn't get married when the day came because the rings were missing! So, we ended up eloping in a courthouse. And then, a month later, I found the rings in the basement, near mysterious footsteps. The ghosts must've stolen them." Justine pounded her hand with her palm.

"Justine, don't tell anyone about this," Rose said, sitting down. "The girls at my psychic shop wouldn't understand, especially since you're related to Terra. She killed Fern by accident and haunted me for a while. I had to destroy her galvanism machine to stop her from creating zombies. I'll use the money we've made from the shop to pay for our trip to Germany. It'll be easy."

"I understand. I won't tell anyone. When do you think we're going?" Justine asked.

"As soon as possible. Is that okay?" Rose asked.

"Yes, that's fine. I'll be ready. Would you like some dinner?" Justine offered.

Rose agreed, and as Justine prepared the food, the sun dipped below the horizon. They heard a few strange bangs, but continued on.

The plane tickets were booked immediately. Before they left, they still needed to shop, make reservations for Germany, and Rose had to inform the other girls at the shop that she was going to Germany, though she wouldn't tell them the real reason. She'd say she was investigating a haunted castle. It sounded fun, and she honestly thought about suggesting the idea to Justine. But she also wondered what kind of reaction the others—Victoria, Sylvie, and Lana—would have.

Justine didn't mind if Rose wanted to visit a castle. She had wanted to do a bit of sightseeing herself. As Rose weighed the pros and cons, she realized what they were doing felt right. The fennel tea would go inside Justine, and the ghosts wouldn't be able to harm her anymore. Rose could even stay with her afterward, just to be sure there were no lingering spirits. If the ghosts were angry about Justine sending them away, she would be elsewhere. Rose planned to make the fennel into a tea, and Justine could take it home and drink it more than once.

It was all working out. Victoria believed the haunted German castle story, and Justine couldn't wait to go. She seemed to have come back to life a little. There was now something for her to look forward to. She even started contemplating moving into a cheerful apartment.

A Haunted Destination: Part 2

IT DIDN'T TAKE LONG for them to board the plane to Germany. Rose had paid for the plane tickets since this was her idea, and she wanted to take responsibility for it. The ride was long, but in the end, it was worth it. She had brought the fennel herb from America with her and planned to soak it in hot water, then pour it into the gold chalice, which was real gold. The stem was 14k. She took her purse with the map of The Black Forest as they landed. Once on the ground, they grabbed their passports and headed to pick up their luggage.

When they arrived at the motel, they were both eager to eat and rest.

"The bride of Frankenstein came here on her honeymoon," Rose said.

"She wasn't really the bride of Frankenstein," Justine laughed.

Rose laughed as well, but as she looked at Justine, she couldn't help but notice the resemblance. The long black hair with a light gray streak, the dark, Gothic eyes. Justine was petite but in her mid-forties, which explained the streak of gray. She also wore a lot of black and makeup to cover her pale face.

"Tomorrow, we pick up the blessed chalice at a nearby church. We'll borrow it, come back here, make hot tea, and you drink all of it," Rose said. "I think the pope blessed it. They asked if we were baptized. I told them no, so we may have to do that and stay for a church service since we're borrowing the chalice."

"Okay," Justine agreed. "I guess it sounds like a good idea."

The following day, when they arrived at the church, everyone was incredibly friendly. A receptionist took them to a back room with a locked cabinet. When she opened it, they saw the chalice gleaming like the sun. The gemstones were garnets and emeralds.

"This was blessed by a priest who met the pope," the receptionist said, giggling at the thought of the pope's fame. "One day, we'll actually meet the pope."

Rose nodded in agreement, impressed by the significance.

"Will you both be available this Sunday to come to church and get baptized?" she asked.

"Yes, we'll be there," Rose replied. "We'll return the chalice after the service. We won't stay longer than three days."

She realized she had brought enough fennel for both of them to drink, and with that, the ghosts from the castle wouldn't be able to interfere with them.

"Okay, I'll be here. My name is Lisa. Just come to the office, and we'll baptize people after the service."

"Alright, great. I'm Rose Cortez, and this is Justine Anderson. We'll be here. Thank you for the chalice," Rose said.

The woman nodded and handed Rose the chalice like it was the Holy Grail. Not sure how to handle it, Rose cradled it gently, almost like it was her baby. When the woman left, Rose tucked it into her purse.

"Let's get out of here," Justine said, and Rose agreed.

As they drove back to their motel, they admired the beautiful trees and the vibrant leaves that lined the roads. They stopped for a warm meal: steak sandwiches and fries. Afterward, they returned to the motel to rest.

While Rose prepared the tea, she said, "I'll make tea for both of us. That way, tomorrow, none of the ghosts will bother us, and when we get to your house, I can stay with you to make sure they won't hurt me either."

Rose rinsed the chalice with soap and hot water. Then she boiled some water and poured it into the chalice. After waiting a minute, she handed it to Justine.

Justine made the sign of the cross and peered inside. Tea leaves were at the bottom. She smelled it. It smelled like regular tea. It looked good, so she took a slow sip, then drank more quickly. When she finished, she dropped the chalice and waited. The tea had tasted good, and now she felt better. When she glanced in the mirror, her face had more color. Her hair was shinier, and the small gray streak was gone.

Rose stared at her in awe.

"What?" Justine asked, noticing the look.

"You look so healthy, and your hair is shiny," Rose said.

"When I get back, I'm going to see my ex-husband, so he can see what he no longer has," Justine replied, and they both laughed.

Rose picked up the chalice. "My turn," she said. She made the tea and drank it. Immediately, her hair became beautiful and shiny, her complexion flawless, and her lips a perfect cherry red. The scar on her arm from a poltergeist had disappeared.

"Look at you!" Justine exclaimed.

Rose glanced at her reflection. She felt perfect. "Do you want to know a secret?" she asked.

Justine nodded.

"The bride of Frankenstein made zombies that killed my husband. She didn't mean for it to happen," Rose revealed.

"Oh, I'm sorry," Justine said, her expression softening. "At least all that's over now. I don't think her ghost is at my house anymore either."

Rose nodded. "I suspected that. I tried to destroy her. She was no good in death." Rose was beginning to really enjoy Justine's company, but she didn't want to ask her to be a rose in the circle of roses. Hopefully, Justine's troubles were over.

Their next assignment was a haunted castle in the Black Forest of Germany. It was old and stood alone, probably home to some unfriendly ghosts. The crumbling bricks at the edges gave it a sinister look. They parked their rented car and began walking toward the castle. Justine surveyed the bare trees, which made the place look even more eerie. Rose grabbed the large front door and pulled. It barely budged, so she pulled with both hands. It creaked and groaned as she forced it open.

They heard wings flapping, and two black bats flew out from the door. The sun sank lower in the sky.

"Hello?" Rose called out. A loud bang came from the other side of the castle. Quickly, she turned on her camera light. Both women were dressed in black with long coats to conceal themselves from any ghosts that might be lurking in the night. They only needed to confirm that the place was actually haunted, and then they could leave.

Another sound boomed through the castle. "What was that?" Justine asked, her voice trembling.

"A ghost, I'm sure. We'll stay another thirty minutes. It's haunted, and I want to get out of here. Someone actually went missing, and they were last seen outside this castle," Rose whispered.

Justine nodded in agreement. They moved cautiously, searching for stairs, but soon stumbled upon something strange. It was a pile of leaves—and a dead bird. As they entered a new room, they noticed scratches on the walls and chains hanging from the ceiling.

"What is that from?" Justine asked, her voice shaking as a chill ran down her back.

"This must have been a torture chamber," Rose said as she surveyed the macabre scene. Justine's lip quivered, and Rose, feeling nauseous, leaned against a dark wall. Suddenly, the wall opened, and she jumped back in surprise.

"It's a secret door!" Rose whispered in awe. Shining her flashlight down the hall, she didn't see anything, but the air was thick with the smell of age and mold.

As they slowly entered, the long hallway seemed even more mysterious. What had this place been used for, they wondered. The castle stood, forlorn, isolated by time.

"Rose, let's turn back," Justine said, her voice filled with unease.

"Something's grabbing my arm!" Rose exclaimed. She turned to see if it was a branch, but there was nothing. Panic surged through them as they both bolted down the hallway. Their hearts pounded in their chests, and they kept glancing behind them as the walls seemed to close in.

When they turned around, they saw someone—or something—in the form of smoke coming toward them. But it wasn't just one figure; now there were five. All they could do was run. They sprinted toward the exit, but when they stepped outside, it was dark. A thick, foggy mist surrounded them. It was so dense they couldn't even see the car. Thunder rumbled in the distance, and rain threatened, though it hadn't started yet.

"We need to get to the car," Rose said, her voice urgent.

"Are they following us?" Justine asked, her breath ragged.

Rose glanced behind them. One of the smoke figures had emerged from the castle and was staring at them. They both ran faster, but still, they couldn't reach the car.

They ducked behind a tree, panting heavily. The ghost didn't follow them but rustled through the trees instead.

"I'm glad we wore black today," Justine whispered, her voice shaky.

"Yeah, but where's the car?" Rose looked around frantically but couldn't see it. They crept quietly, moving cautiously through the mist, but still, no sign of the car. They returned to the castle and started feeling around, hoping to find something familiar.

Justine grabbed something cold and firm. "I've got an arm!"

"Is it a ghost?" Rose asked, fear creeping into her voice.

"No, it feels like flesh," Justine replied, her breathing heavy with panic. "Where the heck is the car?"

Rose ran forward quickly, then suddenly hit something metal. "The car!" she exclaimed. They both jumped in and locked the doors. Rose turned on the headlights and backed out, her hands trembling slightly as she did.

"Where are they?" Justine asked, her voice shaky. Just then, they saw a smoky ghost to their left. When it spotted them, Rose slammed the car into gear, spinning the wheel, and sped off, her heart pounding.

Justine was stunned at how fast the ghost could move, but once they hit the road, they managed to lose it. "That arm I felt by the tree... it had no pulse. And it was so cold. It was the missing person. We have to report it."

"After we get baptized tomorrow and return the chalice, we'll go home the next morning," Rose reassured her, keeping her eyes on the road.

When they finally made it back to the motel, Rose immediately called to report everything. The two women were like heroes when the missing woman was found. Rose called her mother, explaining what had happened. Her parents were as supportive and calming as always.

"I have to make sure she's okay, Mom," Rose said softly.

"I know, sweetie. Just call us when you get home, alright?" her mother replied.

"I will. That was a nightmarish scene. I'll leave the bathroom light on tonight," Rose murmured before hanging up. She tried to relax as they ate dinner, her thoughts lingering on the church. That haunted castle had felt like stepping back in time. It was nothing like Chicago. She couldn't wait to get back. Once they did, she planned to spend a night with Justine to make sure she was okay. Then, soon enough, it would be time to face the roses. They'd want to know what happened, but they didn't know about Justine's connection to monsters. Rose felt sure it wasn't her fault. Justine was a good person—someone deserving of love, peace, and happiness. She actually looked forward to Justine's house.

"My house is probably clear now. And if it is, I don't think I'll move. I'll just redecorate!" Justine smiled, picking up the magazine she had been reading.

"Those ghosts aren't anywhere near us," Rose reassured her. "Wouldn't it be terrifying if we got to your house and they were still there?" Rose laughed at the thought and, exhausted, passed out on the bed.

Justine opened the refrigerator door. There was just enough to make a sandwich and a simple dinner for the night. "I'll go to the store first thing tomorrow morning," she told Rose.

The house felt heavy with dust, and the gray exterior only added to the depressing atmosphere. It was time for a change.

By nightfall, they were both on edge, listening intently for any sounds. "There are no ghosts left," Justine called out from her room, trying to reassure them both.

Rose wasn't convinced. She went out for a drink and, as she walked past the stairs, heard a clank from the attic. A ghost. The attic door creaked open on its own. She didn't want to alarm Justine, but the sound was unmistakable.

"What was that?" Justine called from her room.

"It's a ghost," Rose replied. "I think there's one hiding in the attic. I'm going to hang fennel in your doorway. They won't bother you then. They're stubborn, hard to get rid of. I'll do it now."

After Rose hung the fennel, everything fell silent. But she couldn't shake the feeling that something was wrong. Just as she was starting to relax, she saw the bride of Frankenstein's ghost pass by the window. It was too quiet now—probably because Justine was away. "Why do you haunt your family?" Rose whispered.

"I want to be here. I want to be scary, but respected," Terra, the ghost, answered, her voice an eerie whisper.

By morning, Justine seemed resigned. "It's okay that this house is haunted by Terra. I want to get an apartment anyway."

"They can follow you," Rose warned, glancing at the door, half-expecting the ghost to return.

"I'll take my chances. I bet if I sell the house, they'll bother the new owners instead," Justine said with a shrug.

"I don't know," Rose replied, thoughtful. "Terra last night said she wanted you. Maybe she won't find you for a while." Rose tried to gauge what the ghosts would do next. "Can I spend the night again? I want to observe the ghosts and see if I can talk to one."

"Sure, stay as long as you need," Justine said. "But I'm going to pack some stuff today. I'll apply for an apartment, then put the house up for sale later."

"That's perfect. I'll stay here. Maybe I'll even rent it from you. What do you think? I'll keep an eye on the ghosts and make sure they don't come after you. Just kidding, but I'll try," Rose joked.

"Sounds great," Justine said. "It's perfect."

"This won't just be landlord and tenant. We'll be close friends," Rose said with a smile. "At the shop, we have Sylvie, a young girl covering for her mother, and Victoria, an experienced ghost hunter. Victoria's quiet, but Lana, Sylvie's mom, had an accident. Both of her legs are broken, so she won't be back for a while."

"I'd like to meet them," Justine said.

"Of course. Just don't tell them you're related to the bride of Frankenstein," Rose teased.

"Okay," Justine laughed. "I'm going to the store. I'm buying a ton of groceries for us. I'm the assistant manager at a nice restaurant, so I don't have to work for a couple of days. I also need to trim my hair so I can comfortably wear it in a ponytail." Justine grinned, proud of herself.

Rose believed the house would be perfect for her. Once she sold the house she had lived in with Rusty, she would have rent money. The place had potential—it just needed personality and some houseplants.

"I'm not sure what to charge for rent. I've never done this before. How about five hundred a month? If you pay six fifty, I'll throw in utilities," Justine offered.

"That's perfect," Rose smiled. "Let's celebrate. Man, I'll take this house and these nasty ghosts. Oh, and I have a cat named Muffin."

"I don't care. He can't do any harm to this house," Justine said.

"Na, but he can do damage to my furniture." Rose laughed at the cat comment and purred.

Justine got a kick out of it. "I'm going to get wine, cheese, and crackers to celebrate, and tomorrow I can start looking for an apartment."

"Sounds good. I'm going to go back to my house and grab my things. I want to bring my ghost-hunting equipment so I'm ready when they come out. I hope they're not mad we went to Germany and drank that herbal tea," Rose stated.

"Me neither." Justine stood up, grabbed her shoes and purse, and put on her favorite diamond necklace before leaving.

As Rose sat alone, she heard strange noises—just the old house creaking and water dripping. She thought about how she would decorate it. After Rusty died, she had wondered when she would sell their house. Now felt like the perfect time. She grabbed her keys and headed out, ready to pack her suitcase and get everything she needed, including food.

When Justine returned, she had bags of food, but Rose was gone. Getting your belongings could take some time, especially with traffic—it was nearly an hour away. The once chilling house seemed to surrender to new life. At least that's how Justine saw it. It wasn't lonely anymore. It would occupy two people until it had someone new. Someone with a cat that wasn't related to the Bride of Frankenstein.

Justine had seen the house as a curse, a jinx. Maybe the ghost would just give up, maybe it would go away. Or maybe it would attack her before she left—it was possible. She loved her parents and her grandparents, but she never knew her great-grandmother Terra. What kind of person was she? Negligent? The thoughts made her want to talk to her mother. No one cared for her more. Her father was protective. They might be angry if they knew she was haunted.

Justine opened a window and turned on her stereo, craving some civilization. One thing she couldn't decide was how to see her ex again. She wanted him to regret leaving her, but if he was married, she didn't have a chance.

She lay down on the couch, and a cloud of dust billowed up. Next on the agenda: cleaning. She propped her feet up. She was done living like this. An apartment would be nice. She could swim in the pool and do things people liked to do there.

"That was bad traffic," Rose said, opening the door with a loud creak. She had a suitcase and a bag of laundry. After another trip to the car, she returned with a cat in a carrier and a box of personal items. "There's more in my trunk. I just thought I'd grab this for now."

Justine eyed the cat. It was cute and fluffy with long fur. The cat gazed at her with a long, affectionate look. Rose let it out of the carrier, and it slowly crept toward Justine. She gently petted it as it walked around the house, getting familiar with its new surroundings. It disappeared, no doubt to be found later.

"Muffin likes to explore," Rose said.

Rose opened the large circular doors adorned with roses. Victoria and Sylvie were watching.

"The girl I brought to Germany found a dead body in front of the castle," Rose announced loudly. "All we had to do was keep an eye out for the missing girl and make sure it's actually haunted—and we did."

Sylvie clapped. "That's amazing!"

Rose nodded. "Her name is Justine. She had a haunted house, and I didn't want to go alone to another country, so I brought her. No more Germany. I ran from those ghosts." She stared at the ground. "I'm moving into Justine's haunted house. She's renting it to me after she moves out."

Victoria raised an eyebrow. "Are you sure you want to?"

"Yes, it'll take some getting used to," Rose said, perking up. "Besides, I really want to get out of Rusty's old house."

"Alright," Victoria replied.

"How's your mother, Sylvie?" Rose asked.

"She's okay. The casts will be on for another couple of months. Dana wants to work here, but she's still just going to school. She's not depressed anymore."

"That's good," Rose said.

When Rose got home that night, Justine was already there. Muffin sat next to her on the couch.

"I went to visit my mom today. She wasn't happy about the ghosts, but she thought Germany was cool. She also said moving was a good idea. I'm going in the right direction," Justine said.

"What about the ghosts? Did you hear anything strange?" Rose asked.

"Just the house settling," Justine answered. It seemed fine for now.

"I want pizza," Rose said, and Justine nodded in agreement.

Later that night, as they ate pizza, there was a knock at the door. Justine went to answer it, but there was no one there. When she turned around, a large woman with black hair blowing in the wind stood before her.

"Justine, you cannot leave. If you do, we will find you and hunt you," the unearthly voice warned.

Justine jerked at the threat.

"Don't be afraid of her. It's just a threat. Protection herbs will stop her. I have them. She can't touch you," Rose said.

When Justine ate breakfast, she was all alone. She was cat-sitting and had just given Muffin her breakfast. "I got some cat cereal for you," she said as she poured it into a bowl. Muffin purred and rubbed against her hand.

With their bellies full, it was time to go apartment hunting. She put on her best skirt and a silk blouse, ready to see some open apartments. As she dropped her shoes, she heard a small bang in the hallway. "I've got to get out of here," she muttered to herself.

"I applied for one of the apartments I saw today. It's perfect. It's on the second story," Justine said.

"Oh, good. I'd like to see it," Rose replied.

"It's not that far—about fifteen minutes away—and it does have a swimming pool." Justine smiled with excitement.

"I can put my house up for sale, the old shack. Can I paint this house later so it's not so gloomy and gray?" Rose asked, sitting on the bed.

"Yes, go ahead. Because if you don't rent, I'll just sell it."

"I'll call my real estate agent and pack tomorrow. I'll bet they can sell that house quickly, and I'm not going to ask for an outrageous amount of money," Rose said.

The following morning, Rose woke to a moving truck in the driveway. Justine had movers putting all of her furniture into the truck.

"I'll leave you the dining room table, couch, one chair, and living room table. I can't take everything," Justine said.

"I want my bed. It's a nice polished wood bed, and I'll get it today," Rose said, grinning from ear to ear.

"I'll tell you what. When I'm done with the truck, I'll let you use it to get your furniture. That would be easier. I've rented it, so by tomorrow, you'll have it to get everything. And tonight, we'll make a special trip to get your bed," Justine offered.

"That's a great idea," Rose said, her eyes lighting up.

Everything went as planned, and when the girls got Rose's big, beautiful, perfect bed, they both had to move it in. They switched Justine's simple bed for Rose's. The house had a new feel to it. But Rose couldn't shake the feeling that she was being watched.

"You know, my house used to be haunted by two goons who came in through a mirror portal. I'm not going to tell anyone, though," Rose said.

"Okay, we're all set for tomorrow. I'll leave the truck for you and take the car to my apartment. Thank you so much, Rose, for everything you've done." She held out her hand to shake. "You're going to be a great tenant. The rent we agreed on will be due the first of every month."

"You're welcome. It's been nice staying with you. I hope the ghosts and I get along just fine." As she said that, they both heard a banging upstairs and laughed.

"I'll see you tomorrow," Justine said, and she was out the door.

Rose had a different house to live in now, and she wasn't totally alone—she had Muffin. The house looked bare, but it would be great when she got her furniture. Things were going to be different, but the rose cases seemed the same. She tried to forget the ghosts by making them happy. As long as they stayed that way, she sometimes opened a window hoping they would go out, but winter was coming, and it was getting cold. I live in a haunted house again, she thought. I won't tell anyone that the house I'm going to sell was haunted. Maybe I'll let it slip that my husband, who lived there, died. It was quiet until Muffin purred. She was the best. Rose unpacked her suitcase and couldn't wait to get the rest of her belongings.

IT WAS PARTICULARLY cold that December night, and snow was sure to follow soon. As Rose sat on her couch next to her heater, she stared up at her tree. It wasn't decorated yet, but she thought it would look nice in blue, green, and silver. She needed to shop for a big silver glittery star for the top. She put her multicolored lights on it and plugged them in—beautiful. The pine smelled wonderful.

The house looked a lot better since Justine moved out. The outside had been painted white, and she had put her old house up for sale. Once her new house was painted, vacuumed, and all of Rose's furniture was put in (which wasn't much), it looked clean and new. Her houseplants gave it life.

Her psychic cat, Muffin, began pawing at the air. Rose watched her walk away into another room, where she mewed a lot. When the cat screamed, Rose came running. Rose's crystal ball was lit up with a head inside. Its hair looked like dreadlocks, its neck severed and dripping with blood. The hair was dirty.

"Who are you?" Rose asked. Her cat stared, its hair standing up.

The ghost head flew into the room from out of the crystal ball. It bobbed in the air and flew out the window.

Rose ran to the window and looked out. It was gone! It was a dark, still night with bare trees and a bright moon. "Medusa!" she called. It reminded her of Medusa, so she made a note to look for the Medusa ghost.

She waited for the ghost to return, and soon it did. One thing Rose hated was ghosts in her bedroom, and that had happened. One night, she woke in the middle of the night and saw it watching her sleep. Except this time, it had a body. She could see through it. The ghost was dirty.

She flipped on a light, and it stared at her. Rose asked, "What do you want?"

It stared as if it wanted to talk. Her lips moved, quivering slightly.

"Are you coming in from upstairs?" Rose asked, trying to get it to talk.

The ghost shook its head.

"Are there others?" Rose asked.

It shook its head again. Just then, the ghost pointed to the window.

Rose looked out the window and didn't see anything. All she saw were mounds of wet dirt from the rain. She looked back at the ghost. When Rose got up to leave, her bedroom door slammed shut, blocking her path. That was it! One of them was probably her grave mound. Looking out the window, she saw a long mound in the distance with rocks on it. She shivered internally..

She had to wait until morning to dig it up—or better yet, call the police to do it. She called them to report a grave mound, mostly hidden by trees and brush, and told them it could be the missing girl they had been searching for! That would keep the ghost satisfied for now.

Rose didn't want to go out in the dark, but more than one officer arrived, and they had flashing lights and large flashlights. Rose turned on the yard lights for them. They began digging. She stepped away from the window.

When they uncovered the body, it was mostly bones, but the skull still had hair clinging to it—muddy as ever. Rose ran outside. "Medusa!" she called.

"What?" an officer asked. There were several of them.

"I saw her ghost, and she reminded me of Medusa. I'm so glad you found her. Now she'll find peace. She was a good ghost. Do you know who she is?"

"Not a clue," the officer answered. "But we'll never stop searching, and she will be laid to rest."

"Well, please keep me updated," Rose said.

They nodded in agreement. "We're going to be patrolling the area. There's a serial killer out there, and this could be his victim. He's an escaped lunatic. Keep your doors locked, and trust no one," the officer advised.

"I just moved out here last month. I'll get a burglar alarm. That's a great idea!" Rose clapped her hands together. "Floodlights, too. The only other houses are five minutes away." She shook her head. It was peaceful out here, but Rose didn't like the idea of a maniac being so close.

"It looks like this woman's been dead a while. He could be long gone," the officer told her. He handed her his business card. "Call us if you need us."

The kiss of death, Rose thought. What else could be out in these woods? Witches, ghosts, creepers? Rose said, "Thank you, officers," and went inside. She locked the door. "Hello?" she called to the ghost. "Is anyone here?" Nothing answered. The ghost was too quiet. She sat on the couch by her heater and nightlight. She planned to go to bed at sunrise, but accidentally fell asleep on the couch.

When Rose woke the next morning, she felt better but was still worried about the murderer. Heck, she thought, he's probably long gone. No need to flee. Then a thought occurred to her: What if the cops wanted Justine's name? Would she get mad at Rose and evict her? What if her ex-husband had done the killing, and Justine never told because she couldn't? Was her ex wanted?

There was no way she was calling Justine to ask. Somehow, the police would figure out who Rose was renting from. Either way, she guessed the Andersons knew who had killed her, and that probably made the ghost very angry. She chuckled at how quiet the house was. As they both expected, Justine's ghosts had probably found her at her new apartment and were crammed in there, sometimes. The thought of strange occurrences in that apartment made her smile—a sudden appliance turning on, a door closing by itself, things moving on their own. Medusa was probably heading there now because she had been killed by a Medusa killer who preyed on people like her.

The cops called the following evening with shocking information. The woman's name was Cheri Day, and they had taken Justine Anderson to the station for questioning. Justine had confessed to everything. She was guilty of obstructing justice, but it wasn't her ex-husband who killed Cheri; it was her ex-boyfriend. That was another reason nobody wanted to go to her house. Cheri had gone missing, and the last place she was seen was at Justine's house, one year ago, at her Christmas party.

◈ The Party, One Year Earlier ◈

The party was formal. They had dinner, music, and someone brought drugs. There were a lot of people there, and some were exchanging Christmas gifts. Justine had a lot of eggnog. Her ex, Joe, had been invited, and she had a date named Terry. Terry was tall, lean, and had saved a lot of money. The tree was big and beautiful.

Justine really liked Joe, but it didn't work out because he worked a lot and was crabby. He barely had time for her, and he drifted away. As she stood, watching her party in her black and gold dress, she spotted Cheri talking to Joe. Justine was over him, and it was fine. She grabbed a glass of wine, and he popped a drug into his mouth. Cheri wasn't looking, so she went to the backyard. She waited for him, and he came.

Justine thought, good riddance, and she went to mingle and laugh with her date.

It was very cold outside, but the girls were wearing thick winter dresses. They drank their wine and walked toward the trees. Cheri's eyes were getting tired, and Joe looked drunk. He stared at her and noticed she was wearing a large diamond ring. He grabbed her hand and tried to kiss her on the cheek. She tried to slap him, but instead, she scraped his face with the ring. Joe knocked her over, sarcastically screaming "sweetheart" over and over, and she hit and kicked, her head aching. She began kicking him with her heel, digging the points into his leg. He hit her back, frowning, and she staggered. When she screamed, he shook, gagged her with his handkerchief, and strangled her. The light went out of her eyes as she stared at the stars.

When he saw what he had done, he began covering her body with branches and ran into the house. He walked, panicking, to the kitchen and threw up in the sink.

"What's wrong?" Justine asked.

"I've had wine and drugs. My stomach hurts. Also, Cheri is outside. She's passed out cold." He motioned for her to follow him outside. She followed him twenty feet to Cheri's body, which lay there with her eyes staring straight up.

"What will the cops say?" The music played loudly inside. "We have to hide this." In agreement, he followed her to the side of the house, where she grabbed two shovels.

He began digging a grave for her in the trees.

"Wait, don't you think we ought to cover her first? Out of respect?" Justine asked.

"Yes, okay," he said. "You go get a blanket, and I'll keep digging."

She ran inside and grabbed a thick blanket. As she hurried back to him in the trees, her dress caught on a thorny branch and tore.

She took off her shoes, and they both dug. They wrapped her up and rolled her in. They covered her with dirt, rocks, and brush.

"Don't tell anyone," he said. "Or they'll be calling me 'Killer Joe.'"

"I won't," she said, crossing her heart.

The party went on as usual. Everything did. People looked for her, but no one knew what had happened to her. Christmas Day came and went, but there was no Cheri. She was deeply missed, but Justine was too afraid to tell. Cheri didn't start haunting the place until Rose lived there alone. She had rested peacefully.

People found out she had died and remembered her as a happy person. They called her "Cheery Day." Joe confessed to killing her, but claimed it was only because he was on drugs. She was a lovely lady, and he had been thinking about dating her. The police believed him and thought he hadn't killed anyone, until he was connected to a few more bodies. He kept killing, enjoying the power. When one of his victims hit him to get away, he was very unhappy. He stared in pain as the man ran away, screaming for help down the street. Justine did not know he had kept killing. Now she was caught and waiting for a prison sentence. She would likely get at least twenty years.

Rose wondered how she would pay the rent, or if she should just move. In the end, she decided to pay it by sending a check. It turned out to be her last check because Rose had made up her mind to move. She would do it right after Christmas. Cheri's ghost was still around, probably waiting to move on. Her case had been solved after a year— a long time to be dead, not found, or heard. She was a good ghost, but Rose didn't know what to do anymore about living with her. She didn't want to tell the roses about what had happened. Rose and Cheri's ghost continued to live together until Rose figured out what to do and where to go.

Her house hadn't sold, and one day, not long after, on a bad day, she picked up her cat and went back to her old home, wanting to stay for a little while. She found peace in the quiet, with the wind, flowers, and no Justine.

"SYLVIE, IT'S TIME FOR my doctor's appointment to get my casts off!" Lana called up the stairs.

"Okay." Sylvie came down, putting on her gloves. It was frosty outside from the January cold. "I called Dad to tell him, and he was so happy you were feeling better." She picked up her purse.

"After all that aching in my legs, it's time to get the casts off." Her nurse, CeCe, handed her the crutches.

Both Langlys stared at her, as if ready to burst and say goodbye. "It was great having you," Sylvie said.

"Thank you for all of your help," Lana said softly.

"You're welcome. I'll follow you to the hospital, and I'll resume work there while you get your casts removed. It's been a nice stay here, and remember, don't forget to call my nurse's number if anything feels off." Nurse CeCe helped Lana out the door and into the car.

As Lana sat, she waved to CeCe through the car window and forced a smile. She liked her, and the nurse had been a big help.

Sylvie got into the car.

"Did your father say anything nice about me?" Lana asked.

"Just that he hoped you'd get better." Sylvie started the car.

"Did he say he's lost weight or anything?" Lana asked.

"No. Why?" Sylvie stared at her.

"I was wondering if we'll ever date again," Lana said sheepishly.

"Oh, I don't know. He doesn't have a girlfriend. Not since Rachel died," Sylvie answered.

"Maybe he'll lose weight. Would you like to see us get back together?" Lana asked.

"I don't know. Sure, why not. You could try. I don't know how to help," Sylvie said, pulling out of the driveway.

"We'll think about it," Lana said, reclining her seat and relaxing.

The hospital wasn't too far, but the wait to see the doctor was a little long. "What's taking so long?" Lana said.

"Read a magazine." Sylvie handed her one.

"My legs are hot, cooked, and ready to come out of the casts."

"I'll bet," Sylvie said.

Lana rubbed her casts. "I can't wait for them to get out here and saw these off," she said loudly.

An elderly woman sitting across from her looked up. "I have just the thing for you," she said softly, pulling something out of her purse. She handed Lana a business card. "This is a good place. They will help, and the herbs will make you feel amazing."

"Thank you," Lana said. She looked at the card. It read: Greener-house Apothecary. For all your natural needs. We do miracles. Lana didn't think they really did miracles; it was just a sales pitch. But since her accident, she hadn't gotten enough sun, enough exercise, and she hadn't been taking care of herself. She wanted all the help she could get.

The door opened, and a nurse called, "Lana Langly."

"It's time," Lana said, disappearing inside.

The doctors were right—it was time for the casts to come off. As the doctors cut through them, Lana thought about freedom. "Should I walk with a cane?" she asked.

"No, you're better. You need to get used to walking without them. Start slow, then gradually go faster," the doctor said.

"Okay. My daughter is driving me home," she said, and the doctor nodded with approval. "I'll be driving in no time." When the casts were off, Lana stood and slowly moved her legs. "I'll do my own physical therapy. I'll go for walks, then run. I'll get exercise. And I want to try herbs."

"That's a great idea," the doctor said approvingly.

Slowly, Lana walked out of the office. When Sylvie saw her, she ran to her and hugged her. The first thing they did was stop for lunch to fill up Lana's stomach.

It didn't take long for Lana to get moving again. By the weekend, both of her daughters had helped her walk and applauded at how well she did it. "It's just one foot in front of the other," Lana said.

Dana nodded in agreement, then stood up and walked too. Sylvie did the same and bowed. They all laughed. "I can drive, and there's somewhere I want to take the car."

"Alright," Sylvie said.

"I didn't get out much with two legs broken," Lana said. "How's school, Dana?"

"It's going well. I think I'll major in medical reception."

"That's a good idea. What do you guys want for dinner tonight?" Lana asked.

"I bought a big box of enchiladas. I can make it," Sylvie said. "I want to save money working at the Circle of Roses and buy a car. Dana and I can both drive it."

"That sounds like a good idea. I want to go back to the Circle of Roses someday," Lana said.

"I want to be there too," Dana added. She thought it was a good idea—maybe after she graduated.

"I want to walk over to Dana's school tomorrow and see her classrooms. I'm interested in studying criminal law, parapsychology, and office procedures," Sylvie said.

"Good. I'm going to that Greener-house Apothecary to see what I can find. I want to build strength," Lana said.

"Protein and juice, Mom," Sylvie said, offering her advice with a smile.

"You're right, but I still want to check it out. It's in the middle of nowhere, in a small town just outside of Darling. It'll feel good to get out." Lana laid down on the couch and relaxed.

The small-town apothecary was easy to find. It was the only building for five miles. Surrounded by so many trees, no other cars were in sight, so Lana decided to explore a little. Walking to the back, she discovered an herbal garden—probably the herbs used for medical remedies.

The woman working there appeared to be in her fifties. She wore a soft gray hat to block out the glare from the windows, a green blouse, and a long brown jacket. She took off her jacket and stared at Lana with dark, intense eyes when she entered.

"Can I help you?" she asked.

"I just got two casts off and want to drink something to make me feel good and strong," Lana said.

"I have just the thing." The woman went to the back and returned with a tall box that looked like tea. Plants were pictured on the front, and Lana assumed it was made from herbs.

"Mix this with hot or cold water. In a few hours, you'll feel good and strong." The woman's name tag read Hildie. It must have been a nickname.

"Thank you," Lana said, looking around the store. All she saw were herbs and supplements.

"I can show you what's best. I can also get you more when you're done," Hildie offered.

Lana walked to the window and gazed outside. "What's out here? I'm from Chicago."

"Not much. On this street, there's a café, gift shops, and a small market. If you ever need anything, just let me know. I'm Hildegard, but my friends call me Hildie." They shook hands. Hildie's desire to be helpful was evident; it was the reason she ran the shop. She had helped many people over the years.

"Of course," Lana said. "I'm Lana. I have two daughters, and I used to do psychic work in Chicago." Her shoulder-length blond hair fluttered as the door opened and another customer entered.

Hildie's gaze sharpened with curiosity. "That's great that you're psychic. It can be very useful to know things. I used to use psychic work to see outcomes. I'm sure I still have that big book on psychic work, and another one on psychic spells. Would you like to see it?"

"Yes," Lana nodded. This felt promising. The woman seemed like an old soul.

Hildie led her to the back room, where she kept her herbs, a recipe book for remedies, and even a cauldron. She had always done everything she could to help people. When each remedy was a success, it was great for business. Word of mouth traveled fast in a small town, and Hildie had been practicing witchcraft since she was a teenager. She pulled a large hardcover book from her bookcase and brought it to the front.

Lana opened it and began flipping through the pages. "This is amazing. I haven't been working in the psychic shop because I broke my legs. I want to start again someday.

"You can keep it, dear," Hildie said with a grin.

"Are you kidding? Thanks, that's amazing. Now I have something to read." Lana gave Hildie an affectionate tap on the arm. As she turned the pages, she noticed the book was old. The cover was dirty, thick, and looked like it was two hundred years old. "Is it really that old?

"Yes, but maybe at most, twenty years," Hildie said.

A man, the next customer, approached, ready to purchase herbs.

Lana scooted out of the way. "I'm going home and will try these herbs soon."

"Okay," Hildie said, waving as she spoke.

"Thanks again," Lana said, heading to her car. She stopped, breathed in the fresh air, then got in.

The man left with his purchase, and as Lana drove away toward the small market, Hildie recited the enchanted words: "Wish I may, wish I might, have this spell I wish tonight. Be strong and immune to everything." She pointed her finger at Lana, and it took effect. A small blue light flickered and vanished with Lana, unnoticed by her.

Lana picked up lunch at the small market. It was cold, but when she drove by a beautiful clearing, she had to stop for a while.

The sun peeked through the winter clouds, and all of nature seemed perfect. There was a pond with a frog and vines with large leaves climbing a tree like a bush. Another bush nearby had red berries.

"I love berries," Lana said. As she picked some, she brushed her hand against the leaves of another vine and felt a sharp scrape. She hadn't meant to touch them. The leaves were green and grouped in threes. That woman had been odd, she thought. Just then, thunder rumbled in the distance, and Lana tried to sit while looking up at the clouds. But as she did, she stumbled into the vines! She panicked, feeling them wrap around her, a strange sensation. She rolled from side to side, becoming tangled. Getting up immediately, she ripped off the last vine and threw it, feeling offended.

Rain started to fall, and she dropped everything, rushing back to her car. As she drove, wet and uncomfortable, she scratched her arms. Irritated, she thought about putting ointment on them.

The first thing she did when she got home was apply the ointment, then mixed the drink and drank the whole glass.

When she turned on the bathroom light, she noticed red spots on her arms. But as she got closer, they disappeared. What was in that drink? Later, as she went to bed, the itching returned, and the red spots reappeared, only to vanish again when she walked to the bathroom.

The next morning, she kept it from her daughters, but when she described the plant, Dana said, "That's poison ivy, Mom."

Not good news. "What do you do about that?" She started scratching again.

When the girls went to get something for poison ivy, Lana felt uncertain. That night, while cooking dinner, she was slicing cucumbers when Sylvie suddenly came through the door. Lana glanced up at her, and in that moment, her finger got in the way of the knife. A long cut appeared, but as Lana watched, it disappeared.

"Sorry, Mom." Sylvie kept trying to look at the cut, but Lana hid her hand.

Lana covered the spot where the cut had been, but it healed suddenly. "Sylvie, it's nothing."

Sylvie went on helping with dinner, and it seemed like everything was fine.

As Sylvie took over the cooking, Lana picked up the box of special herbal tea from the apothecary and tucked it into a cabinet so her daughters wouldn't drink it. Her healing rate was abnormal, and she left the kitchen, wishing she had never gone to that store.

There was nothing she could do now but pour out the tea and report the business. But who would she tell? That an apothecary made her heal at an extraordinary rate? The police? A witch? The Circle of Roses? The thought made her stomach sink because she no longer felt like she knew them—except for her daughter. She knew she'd have to check out the store again, but she couldn't throw it out just yet. A witch... it made sense. She had to be a witch, running her business this way. But at the moment, Lana had no one to confide in. All she had was her daughter and her beautiful hair, which had grown while she had been on crutches. She couldn't bring herself to cut it.

Lana decided it was best to return to the store. But when she walked in, Hildie was there and said, "There are no returns. Sorry."

"Are you sure?" Lana asked, wondering if returning the tea would reverse the spell.

"No, I can't. See the sign." Hildie pointed to a sign that read, No Refunds, No Exchanges. New customers wandered in, and Hildie went to greet them. "If you'll excuse me, I have to help them."

Lana watched as Hildie handed the new customers what they needed and gave them a brief tour of the shop. After a while, they left.

Quickly, Lana slipped into the back room and started looking around. The first things she noticed were a cauldron and a recipe book. Piles of books were scattered on the floor, and some of them were spell books. It was clear now—Hildie was a witch, enchanting remedies for her customers. Lana put the open box of herbal tea on the counter. The back room was a mess. There was a broom hanging on the wall, probably just for decoration, and in the cupboard, Lana spotted a witch's hat. But the most shocking thing of all was the frog in a glass case. It was wearing a tiny hat, and beside it, there was a pile of clothes. The name tag on the case read Shane. It looked like a customer who had been turned into a frog—or maybe it was meant to represent her customers. Lana quickly grabbed what she wanted and hoped she would never have to come back.

When she heard more customers enter, she left the store and sat in her car across the street, watching, waiting to see what would happen. Eventually, as customers made their purchases, Lana saw Hildie point at one of them and cast a spell. The customer turned into a mouse. Hildie picked it up and took it to the back room.

Another customer arrived, and Hildie pointed a wand at him. It was just a stick of wood, but she cast a spell nonetheless. This had to stop. Lana didn't know of any witch hunters. The last group of customers left, complaining that one of them had felt something hit her back, and it hurt. Lana had no choice but to leave. She didn't know what the witch would do to her for staring, but she had to go home

As Lana drove away, she noticed a customer exiting the store, wearing a red shirt and a black hat. But when she glanced back, he was gone—she couldn't see him anywhere. As she continued driving, she caught sight of him again in the back seat of her car. His hat was off, and his skin was pale as a sheet. He looked about eighteen, wearing a red polo shirt.

She slammed on the brakes and whipped around. But he was gone!

Where did he come from? He could have been one of Hildie's victims, or perhaps he'd come through a portal, like from a Ouija board or a mirror. Lana also remembered the necromancy book she'd seen in the store. She didn't know much about it, but it seemed to fit. She'd have to keep an eye out for the ghost in case he followed her home.

Back at the store, Hildie put on her witch's hat. When a customer headed toward the door, she pointed her finger at him, hoping to catch him off guard. But she was a bad shot. The spell hit the glass door, ricocheted off the mirror she had hung, and shot back toward her. The blue light from the mirror struck Hildie, freezing her like a popsicle.

The customer, seeing what had happened, laughed and approached her. He reached out and touched her, and she shattered into a million pieces, like a fragile doll.

He wandered into the back room and picked up the frog in the glass case. As he walked toward the door, he turned the sign to "Closed" and gently placed the frog down in the dirt. He wondered, would anyone ever know what had happened here? Either way, he hoped he would never see another enchantress again..

"SYLVIE, DO YOU WANT another assignment?" Rose asked.

"Yes," Sylvie replied. "What is it?"

"A haunted old house with a mean ghost. They want us to get rid of it so they can sell the place. The last owner left, and now they want it cleansed for the next buyer."

"That's fine. How should I do it?" Sylvie asked.

"There are many ways," Rose said. "I would start with herbs and white candles—lots and lots of herbs. I'll get you a ton," Rose said, smiling. "You can come with me to shop for them if you want."

"Okay," Sylvie nodded.

"I'm heading to that big store with the nursery. They have so many different herbs. I used them for Justine's case, and she drank them when we went to Germany. There were still ghosts, but they had no power. I wish we had traps. We could do that—put herbs in a box, and when the ghost goes inside, it snaps shut. But they can move through walls, though."

The day of the cleansing arrived, and Sylvie loaded twenty herb plants into the back of her car. Rose wished her good luck, and she headed toward the haunted south side of Chicago.

The real estate agent, Gina, had unlocked the door but wasn't there. She had left a note: the ghost was upstairs, and she wanted to know how it went. "Alright," Sylvie said to herself.

She turned on her ghost box detector and tape recorder and began walking around the first floor. Nothing. The bright sunlight poured through the windows, lighting up the bare, furniture-less rooms. Dust floated in the empty air. Then, suddenly, a small bang came from the third-story room. It was the darkest part of the house, and the shades were pulled down tightly.

On the second story, there wasn't much—just bedrooms, bathrooms, and plain white walls. She climbed the next small staircase and came to the only door. When she opened it, a dark room greeted her. The drapes were closed on the small window, blocking out all light. Then she heard it—beeps that sounded like Morse code. It was her spirit box, letting her know the spirit was there.

"Hello?" she called.

Suddenly, a mysterious breeze hit her, pushing her back out the door. She slammed into the wall! The door slammed shut in front of her.

Shaking, Sylvie ran down the stairs and called the realtor. "Hi, this is Sylvie Langly. I'd like your permission to plant and hang herbs in this house. It's an effective way of getting rid of ghosts and keeping them out."

"Yes, of course. Is anything wrong?" Gina asked.

Sylvie paused, trying to find the right words. "Yes, I've met the ghost. He's a powerful sucker." Her voice shook. "He blew me out of the door and locked it. So, for this time, I'd like to plant my herbs in the yard. I'll get a plant for the kitchen, but I'll put the rest in the yard and hang the leaves in the front and back doorways. Sound good?"

"Yes, lovely. How long does it take to work?" Gina asked.

"Oh, it depends. I'll come back this Friday to check on it. One thing's for sure, this sucker is strong and definitely upstairs. He locked me out. How will I get back in?" Sylvie asked.

"There's a skeleton key in the kitchen drawer that opens all of the bedrooms," Gina informed her.

"Okay, thanks, skipper." Sylvie hung up and went to find the key.

She used the key to open the door on the third floor. She assumed the door wasn't usually open. "Do you want this door closed?" she asked.

"Yes. Please leave me alone. I heard you downstairs. This is my house now." The voice was thick and male, tinged with sadness.

"I'm sorry. They want me to remove you," Sylvie explained.

"We can make a deal, and I'll try to be quiet," the voice said.

"Okay, who are you?" she asked.

"I have all sorts of nicknames. One's Star, or StarMaster."

The voice seemed to come from the closet. Sylvie sat down on the carpet. "Go on."

"If you let me stay, I'll grant you a wish. What do you want?" Star said.

"Money," Sylvie said, shaking her head in disbelief. She didn't really believe ghosts could grant wishes.

"Money it is. I'll get your ghost-hunting job booming. I'll make sure ghosts are haunting everywhere, and people will need to call you. You'll get so much work, and I can call your manager and request a raise and a big bonus. I can make the money appear on your check. Do you want eight thousand dollars?" Star asked.

"Yes," Sylvie said, still stunned.

"Okay. It's done. Just leave me here. I like it here, and at night I wander free. My night vision is fantastic."

"Alright, but I have to plant a few herbal plants outside. I told Gina I would do it," Sylvie said.

"I heard. There will be plants everywhere. Bring one in, but don't use the ones that get rid of spirits," Star advised.

"Perfect. You want to stay, and I need money. I wasn't sure what to tell Gina if I left without getting rid of you, and what would I tell my manager Rose? I don't know if I can lie," Sylvie said. "Nobody will get hurt, will they?"

"I don't think so. You'll have to tell Rose that you took the plants and tried," Star replied.

"What should I do with the herbs that work?" Sylvie asked.

"Plant them somewhere else," Star said. "Now, will you hold your hand in the air and pretend to shake?"

"Yes." Sylvie complied. "I have to go outside now. Time to start planting." She stepped out of the house with all the plants. All of them were meant to get rid of spirits. She had to go buy all new plants that weren't herbs. She took the herbal ones and hid them in the bushes in her backyard.

Soon, business was booming. Sylvie kept her job only to keep an eye on Star, but it wasn't long before the announcement came.

"You've been doing so well; you're all getting raises," Rose said.

The money came in exactly when Star had promised, and Sylvie began looking for her own apartment.

Then, the message came.

"Sylvie, the ghost isn't gone! I tried to sell the house, and it chased them out. You have to try again."

I can't believe this, Sylvie thought. She immediately called Gina. "I'll try again. This time, I'll fight him harder," she said through clenched teeth.

Sylvie went to the realtors, got a key to the house, and headed over. It was mid-afternoon when she arrived, and she found Star in the closet again. This time, she could see it clearly. It had long fingernails and sharp teeth, its eyes glowing yellow.

"I have to take back this deal. Gina is trying to sell this house. Go into the light," Sylvie demanded.

"I can't do that. Those wages are yours. You need to keep your end of the deal. I won't bother you anymore. I'll stay quiet and let Gina sell the house," Star said.

"Promise?" Sylvie asked the demon.

"I promise. I'll try to live with these people," Star swore. "But if I leave, I'll have to haunt someone. I'll choose you and your family. You might as well take the money and go."

The thought unsettled her. She quickly went to the door, ran down the stairs, and left as fast as she could. This task would have to be passed on to someone else. If Gina called again, she'd have to tell her she was handing it off to another ghost hunter.

Sylvie returned to her room, collapsed on her bed, and reached under the mattress to pull out her diary. She grabbed a pen from her desk and began to write:

Diary Entry

I actually just made a deal with a demon. I wanted to make more money, so I just did it. It's dishonest, but I hid the herbs in some plants outside and planted something else at the house. Gina and Rose know the ghost is still there. I know they want it gone, so when I tried again, it threatened my family. I didn't know it was a demon, but I don't want it following me here. I must tell Rose I'm quitting. What will she think? Well, I'm new, and I need help. Sometimes I'm not sure what methods of ghost-ridding work and which don't. I don't want anyone to know. I could get fired, but I don't think she will fire me. I don't want my family terrorized. They're downstairs making dinner. I never want to see Star again. It hurt when I hit the wall that time he blew me back! I can only hope everything will be okay. Maybe I should read the Bible. Until the next entry. – S..

"Why?" Rose asked, concerned.

"I can't get rid of it. I'm not experienced enough. It threw me into a wall the first time, then nagged me not to plant herbs. The second time, it said it would leave, but then it threatened to target my mother and sister. Honestly, it's evil."

"I understand. Victoria and I will take the assignment. We can find you some ghost hunting jobs, but no ghost-exterminating jobs for now. How does that sound?" Rose asked on the phone.

"That's perfect," Sylvie responded.

"You can also spend your hours working in the store. Now, I'm going to see about getting rid of that evil spirit. We'll need holy water, herbal leaves, and a water gun. I have an idea," Rose said.

"I have the key. You'll need it. I'll drop it off," Sylvie offered.

"Okay, thanks."

"What are you going to do?" Sylvie asked.

"I'm going to make tea out of that spirit that messed with you," Rose said firmly.

"I'm glad you understand. Bye." Sylvie chuckled as she hung up the phone. Sometimes, Rose was the best.

The next evening, Rose and Victoria arrived at the empty house. Rose had mixed herbs with holy water and loaded it into a water gun. The gun was meant to shoot far, giving her a better range. She also carried a flashlight, rosary beads, and a recorder. If something happened to her, maybe someone would find the tape and know what went on. She hit record.

They left the lights off, walking through the house. Everything looked as clean as ever, but they didn't find anything unusual. Rose pulled out the squirt gun. "I'm going up to that third room. Sylvie said it hides in the closet."

She opened the door to the third floor, and still, nothing. She opened the closet door and began squirting the holy water around. Suddenly, a loud growl echoed behind her, and the door slammed shut.

The wind threw her into the wall, and she dropped the water gun. Stumbling, she grabbed her flashlight and turned it on. Slowly, she looked into the closet. She picked up the water gun and sprayed it around the room and in the closet. Silence.

She glanced out the window. Then, she felt a sharp scratch on her upper arm. Three deep claw marks appeared. Instinctively, she reached for her rosary, clutching it tightly. She whispered, "By this power, leave," over and over.

The window shattered, glass flying everywhere, as a fierce gust of wind swept through the room. The wind howled louder, and leaves blew in from outside. It seemed like the storm was intensifying.

It turned into a full-blown windstorm. The trees swayed violently, some of them looking as if they might snap. Rose hoped the demon had left. She had never dealt with a demon before. The lights in the house flickered on and off. Rose dashed down the stairs.

"Come on. Let's get out of here. I think it's gone. I'll have to explain the window to Gina, though," she said, urgency in her voice.

"Just tell her it's an evil spirit," Victoria suggested.

They sprinted to the car. Victoria climbed in, but Rose stopped for a moment, grabbing a potted herb—Angelica—which was known to ward off evil. She placed it by the front door. The wind started to die down, and she quickly joined Victoria in the car. They sped off.

"I don't know if I want to fight demons for a living. Maybe I should go to college," Rose murmured, glancing out the window.

"Good plan, but don't you love being a psychic?" Victoria asked, glancing behind her at the road. The lights in the house had stopped flickering.

"I do, and I want to keep my shop. We fight ghosts, not demons. Maybe this won't happen often. I feel like we're in a movie," Rose said with a chuckle.

"If the demon's gone, why did the lights just flash again?" Victoria asked, furrowing her brow.

"I don't know," Rose replied, her tone uneasy.

"It looks like the flashes are getting farther apart. The house is out of view now. It should just stop. When you talk to Gina, just tell her you think the spirit's gone. There's nothing more they can do," Victoria said, trying to reassure her.

The next day, when Rose explained the situation to Gina on the phone, Gina was not pleased.

"You're ghost hunters. Get rid of it," Gina snapped.

"It's not always that simple. We believe it's a demon," Rose replied, trying to keep her tone calm.

"How do you know it's really gone unless it's completely quiet? And the window is broken—it'll need to be replaced," Gina added.

"Yeah, the window just broke during my fight with the demon," Rose said, glancing at the three claw marks on her arm just above her rose tattoo. "A big windstorm kicked up after that, and I left a plant for protection."

"Okay, fine. Maybe I'll lower the price. I don't think anyone's died there, but I did hear the last people who lived there dabbled in the occult," Gina said, her tone softening a little.

"That's probably it. If you need me, call me," Rose said.

Things settled down afterward. The window in the house was repaired, but the place was never quite the same. No one wanted to buy it. Visitors claimed they had a bad feeling when they stepped inside. Gina eventually decided to rent it out, but even then, people didn't stay long. They didn't see any ghosts, but the atmosphere made them uncomfortable. One man staying there found Satanic items hidden in a small closet. The house just wasn't what anyone was looking for.

"NORMAN OSGOOD IS DEAD. He died of a heart attack at the age of seventy-five. This is the reading of his will. He had many possessions, as a wealthy man would, but the most significant are two million dollars and a mansion that has been in the family for generations. These go to Norman Jr., his first son."

The room was filled with friends and family, but there was no sign of Norman. He was tall and would have been easy to spot. Where was he? Why would he miss his father's will reading? Whispers of disbelief spread through the room.

"If Norman doesn't claim his father's fortune, it will go to Sandy Harrington, his cousin," the lawyer continued, his gaze fixed on the group.

"How long does he have to claim it?" Sandy asked, raising her hand.

"About three months," the lawyer replied. "Let me know his contact information. I'll try to reach him." He nodded as Norman's aunt approached him, handing over the information. The lawyer's name was Emerson, as indicated at the building entrance, but he hadn't used his first name.

Norman didn't answer his phone. His aunt Patty and cousin Sandy knew this immediately when the lawyer called them right after leaving his message.

"We'll go to his house right now," Aunt Patty said, and Sandy quickly followed. Sandy's husband, Randolph, decided to stay home.

As they approached Norman's house, not far from the reading, they saw his car parked outside. They got out and knocked, but there was no answer. They walked around the house, even checking the backyard. Aunt Patty tried the back door—it was locked, but she noticed something unusual: a broken window.

"Norman!" Aunt Patty called as she opened the window. Glass scattered everywhere, and a large rock lay on the floor.

Sandy followed behind, brushing off her black skirt. A breeze swept through the broken window as she called out too, "Norman!"

Inside the house, they saw the mess—papers strewn all over the place. On the couch lay Norman, pale and lifeless. A pool of blood was on the floor. They rushed to him and saw the bullet wound in his head.

Aunt Patty grabbed his phone, her hands shaking. "My nephew's been murdered," she repeated, barely able to steady her voice. She whispered to Sandy, "The police will be here soon."

Sandy stood in stunned silence. Norman had never hurt anyone. Who would want to harm him? She didn't touch anything.

Aunt Patty opened the front door, and they stepped outside to wait. One by one, the authorities arrived—police, investigators, and a coroner. The two women stepped back, watching and listening.

"It doesn't look like anything was stolen," one officer said. "We've got fingerprints, but no suspects yet," another voice added. Norman's body was wheeled away.

Sandy exhaled, her golden blonde hair shining in the sun. "Such a shame my cousin is dead," she murmured. Then, pulling out her phone, she called her husband, Ralph. "Norman's never coming to claim his inheritance," she told him. Her mind raced with thoughts of how they would soon inherit the money. They had always dreamed of a better life, and this money would give it to them. She could go to secretary school, or maybe become a receptionist, instead of working with a dozen screaming kids in a preschool. She imagined what it would be like to live in that mansion. She barely heard Ralph's voice as he spoke to her on the phone.

The reading of the will wasn't a surprise to the couple. They knew Norman Sr. had wealth, and Sandy was next in line because she had always been close to her uncle. She helped him when she could, and he had a soft spot for her. He also loved her mother, and Sandy resembled her. Norman Sr. had been the only one in the family to amass his fortune by starting his own business, which had grown tremendously over the years.

For the time being, the question of why Norman Sr. had been murdered seemed to have an answer: It was because he was an heir. When Sandy returned home, she mulled over whether or not she really wanted the mansion. Ultimately, yes. Her husband, Ralph, wanted to live in it, so she decided to give it a try. She called the lawyer, Emerson and Emerson, to inform them that she would collect the money and keys the following day.

As they packed, Ralph dreamed of the life he always wanted: no work, early retirement at forty-five, and a grand house where he'd sometimes need to search for his wife.

"The lawyer said this house is over one hundred and fifty years old," Sandy said. "We'll have money for the repairs." Though she felt as though the money was all hers, she knew she would have to share some of it with Ralph. What kind of life did she want now? Should she start her own business? Go back to school? She was thirty-eight, younger than Ralph, and now, she'd be wealthy too.

The mansion was probably full of antiques. She would see it in a few days and then decide what to do with it. She laid back on the couch. "In the next few days, I want to get rid of all the old furniture in the mansion and replace it with new stuff. I want to get it from your store."

"That's fine," Ralph replied. "You'll get a discount. I'll also put this house up for sale, and we'll make over a hundred thousand dollars. That money will go into my pocket, and you'll have two million. Maybe we can sell some of the furniture from that old house too," he suggested.

"Yes. Ralph, maybe you shouldn't try early retirement. You'll get bored," Sandy suggested.

"You're right. I'm getting tired of furniture sales. It's a nice business, though. We should get a new bed, Tiffany lamps, and a chandelier. We'll have a beautiful guest room, and everyone will want to stay with us. We can even hire someone to clean the house," Ralph said. "We should attend Norman Sr.'s funeral, out of respect. We did like him."

"But poor Norman Jr.," Sandy said. "Who would do this to him?"

"I don't know," Ralph replied.

Unable to wait, Sandy went to the lawyer's office that afternoon to collect the house address and keys. When she arrived at the mansion, it stood alone, with no other houses nearby. The house appeared gloomy, surrounded by overgrown grass. It sat like a silent observer. She went to the windows and peered inside.

The house was filled with wooden furniture and dust, but it wasn't beyond repair. She opened the front door, feeling almost as though it were magic. The house was spacious—there were about ten rooms. Sandy didn't want to be alone in the house, but she knew her husband would be with her. There was much work to be done, and she wasn't fond of half the furniture. It was clear the house hadn't been cleaned in ages—Norman hadn't bothered, and his wife had passed away years ago from cancer.

The dining room already had a large chandelier, and Sandy turned it on. It sparkled in the dim light. As she walked through the house, she checked the bedrooms. She wanted one on either the second or third floor. Her husband could have his own room. She also wanted to hire a gardener to plant grass, trees, and flowers.

The room she chose was on the second floor, overlooking the front yard. It had a big bed with a blue and white quilt. She lay down on it, not wanting to get up. The room was a mess, and so was the rest of the house. Norman hadn't bothered to hire anyone to clean it during his life..

The kitchen was spacious, with white tiles and white bricks lining the walls. It was a big project. They had to finish packing up their own belongings and then get rid of the old, unwanted furniture in the mansion. Sandy had plenty of family members to give it to.

Everything was going well, but when Ralph saw how much work was involved, he decided to give away most of the furniture to his family too. They came and took it: his uncle, cousin, and sister. It felt like they were starting over, and with the mansion being an hour and a half away, it was bound to be a different life.

As the mansion slowly became cleaner, Sandy decided it was time to call in a gardener. Rolling out the grass took two days, and next came the small trees. But Sandy wanted to pick out the flowers herself. She had a vision for the styles and colors, and she even bought a few plants for inside the house.

Through all the work, she never forgot her uncle's funeral. While at his grave, she said softly, "Thank you for everything."

It had taken her an hour to choose pastel-colored flowers, and she insisted on buying small rose bushes, ones that would eventually grow into large ones.

Ralph picked out his own room, though it was also on the second floor. They hired a plumber and an electrician to make sure everything in the house worked as it should. At night, sometimes Sandy could hear the soft hum of her husband's TV. He didn't have a job, but he kept an eye out for any hiring opportunities.

Strange noises started to come at night, sometimes sounding like pipes rattling. There was also an attic that Sandy hadn't yet dared to explore. She didn't want to.

When she told Ralph, he went up to check it out. "Don't go up there," he said. "It's got dust an inch thick, and there are strange boxes I'm afraid to look at—bugs and mice, probably."

She nodded. "Mice? I haven't heard any."

He shrugged. "It's small. I'm glad we don't have a basement, but this place does have a wine cellar. Let's plant some vines."

Sandy nodded in agreement. Working on the house kept them busy, and by the end, the yard was beautiful, and the house, once gloomy, now stood proud with its mansion-white exterior.

That afternoon, Ralph went to check the mail. Among the usual letters was a square, white, blank envelope. When he opened it, he hoped it would be a welcome note to the neighborhood, maybe with two free tickets to something. But instead, the letter read:

I have written to warn you. This house is cursed. It has been since a woman was pushed down the stairs and killed in the 1800s. The murderer hated her, and after killing her, he cursed the house. Her husband fled, not knowing what to do. I suggest you do the same. Ghosts have haunted this house for years, and there are hardly any animals around. I'm not sure who the ghosts are, but they want to choose the right owner. Take this warning seriously and leave.

The letter was unsigned. There was no address on the front, nor any postmark.

Ralph stood there, thinking for a moment. He knew what he was going to do—but it wouldn't be fleeing. They had just fixed up the house, and they were fine. Whoever was trying to scare them could try harder. Ralph walked toward the house, the note in hand. He wanted to research the woman who had died here and possibly speak with someone—maybe a psychic—to see if the house really was cursed.

He handed the note to Sandy, who was in the kitchen.

She opened it, reading it with a puzzled expression. "It's true. There are no animals here. How will we know if it's cursed?"

"I can find a psychic in Chicago. I'll ask them to figure it out. Until then, let me know if you see anything strange," Ralph said.

That night, Sandy didn't see anything unusual, but she had a bad dream about Ralph. In the dream, he had a knife and was trying to stab someone. He came dangerously close to her, staring at her—but that was all. She woke up, heart racing. When she fell back asleep, she dreamed that Ralph was carrying a gun.

The following day, Ralph left for Chicago, a trip that would take most of the day. The dream kept bothering Sandy, and she couldn't shake the feeling of unease. She decided to search his bedroom and office. Looking through his closet, she found nothing. But in the last drawer of his dresser, she discovered a handgun. She had never known he owned weapons.

Sandy's heart raced as she looked around to see if he had hidden anything else. She rummaged through his laundry basket, and at the bottom, she found his shirt—stained with blood. The stain was brown, dried, and ominous. Sandy felt a chill crawl up her spine. She decided that, when the time was right, she would confront him. But he would be gone for hours, so she busied herself with cleaning, watering the flowers, and grocery shopping.

As she cleaned, a foul smell, like decay, filled the air. She opened several windows to let fresh air in, which helped for a while. The scent of early spring flowers blew in from outside, calming her slightly. She kept thinking about what she would say to Ralph. Would he get defensive?

As she scrubbed the kitchen floors, she heard strange noises upstairs. When she went to the stairs, they stopped. What if it was a residual haunting? she wondered. "Uncle Norman!" she called out.

There was no response. She waited, but the silence stretched on. Taking a deep breath, she decided to go upstairs. When she reached the top, she froze. There, standing at the end of Ralph's bed, was a man. He vanished when he saw her. It was Norman Jr.! It was his father's house.

Another strange thing—Ralph's bed was made. He had never made his bed before. She rushed to her own room. To her surprise, her bed was also made, perfectly straightened. It was as if something—someone—was trying to be kind to her, to help her.

Her heart pounded. She wanted to run, to stay out of the house until Ralph returned. What had he done? She grabbed her purse, deciding that a trip to the grocery store would help clear her mind. Maybe then she would feel better. As she walked toward the front door, she felt a chilling sensation, as though someone were watching her. With a quick breath, she stepped outside, leaving the house behind.

She wondered—was her new fortune blood money?

Ralph didn't return until evening, just as she was cooking soup. The rich aroma filled the kitchen.

"Darling," he said, his voice shaking with worry. "I talked to a psychic named Rose Cortez and showed her the letter. She said it's true—our house is cursed. She also said she'd look into historical records to see if anyone has died here, then give me a call. What should we do?"

Sandy paused, the weight of his words sinking in. "We have to stay. We just sold the old house. We'll wait to hear from Rose. But, Ralph... is it wrong to keep a murdered heir's money?"

He hesitated, his eyes flickering. "No." He inhaled the soup's fragrance, his face softening. "You didn't do anything wrong.""

"I cleaned today. Do you know what I found? You had a few blood spots on a t-shirt. What happened?" she asked.

"I cut myself shaving," he replied, his voice distant, as if struggling to remember.

She nodded, but doubt lingered in her eyes. That night, she would have more unsettling dreams about her husband, and her cousin Norman wandered through them.

Late that night, Sandy heard the phone ring. Ralph answered and soon hung up. He walked into her room, his face tense.

"She said the whole letter is true. A lady died here. That's too bad. She also said strange things, like how a cursed house would try to get rid of me and sees me. She said it would kill until it picked its owner. Maybe someone like my wife. Do you believe that?"

Sandy hesitated, uncertainty clouding her thoughts. "Oh, I don't know if I believe ghosts do that," she replied. Ralph began getting ready for bed.

"Sounds silly," she added, trying to lighten the mood.

He climbed into her bed, and Sandy couldn't help but laugh. He was afraid to sleep by himself.

The next day, Sandy was home alone when the phone rang again. She answered, and it was Rose from the psychic shop.

"How are you doing, Mrs. Harrington?" Rose asked.

"I'm fine. Is this the lady my husband talked to?" Sandy asked, her voice calm but uneasy.

"Yes, I just wanted to check in and see how you both were doing. Also, did they ever find your cousin's murderer? I keep having weird visions of Ralph killing him. I'm not sure what it means," Rose said, her voice laced with concern.

Sandy's stomach churned. "We're okay. My husband thinks this house is haunted. They haven't found the killer yet. No evidence, really. He was shot with one bullet, and the fingerprints didn't lead them to anyone." She hesitated. "I don't know when my husband will be back."

"I just wanted to call and let you know what happened, that's all I can offer at the moment," Rose said, her tone soft.

"Well, thanks. We appreciate it." Sandy hung up the phone slowly, her mind racing. Could Ralph have killed her cousin for the inheritance? She decided to take his bloodstained t-shirt to the police station for analysis. It was the right thing to do. She quickly grabbed the shirt from her closet where she had hidden it and drove to the station.

When she arrived, she said, "I'd like my husband's t-shirt analyzed. He says it's his blood, but I'm not sure. I'm Sandy Harrington, Norman Osgood's cousin."

The officer took the t-shirt. "We'll have this analyzed right away and see if it matches Norman's DNA. It's good that you brought this in. We'll call you, just leave your number with me." He held the shirt in his hands, inspecting it carefully.

The police called before Norman came home. Sandy had just finished eating leftover lasagna when the phone rang, and she dropped it in shock. It took them just ten seconds to tell her that Norman's blood was on her husband's shirt. Ralph had done it. He had shot him up close.

"I'm getting out of here now," she said quietly, her voice trembling.

"Where are you going?" the officer asked, his concern palpable.

"To a quiet inn close by," she answered, her words steady but filled with fear.

"Get as far away as you can. You don't want him to see your car. We're going to your house to wait for him. Call us when you get to the inn so we know you're safe. Don't go back to your house until we arrest him," the officer said, giving clear instructions.

"Yes, I will. He seemed so nice," she murmured, as the realization of her husband's dark secret settled in.

"He's a killer," the officer's voice was blunt, cold.

Sandy hung up, her hands shaking. She went to pack as quickly as she could. She grabbed everything she needed from the bathroom—her pillow, blankets, and anything else she might need for the night. As she packed her suitcase, the weight of what she was about to do settled heavily on her shoulders. She wasn't just leaving; she was fleeing from the man she thought she knew.

She pulled out of the driveway, determined to stay at the most distant inn. She had considered going to the airport hotel and flying to her mother's, but she feared he might look there. She was clever, and he had become a waste of her time. She had first met him at his furniture store while studying to be a preschool teacher.

She drove for over an hour before finding a small, cozy cabin to stay in. He would never find her there. As promised, she called the police station. They still had no updates on his arrest. They asked her where he might hide. If officers were stationed at his driveway, he wouldn't risk stopping to stay there—especially not a murderer trying to cover his tracks. He had murdered his cousin-in-law.

As she sat on the bed, she felt a strange combination of safety and exhaustion. There weren't many other cabins around, and the few cars that were there looked nothing like hers. Maybe he wouldn't find it. Not now. She turned on the bathroom light, shutting the door behind her. The cabin was warm and cozy, complete with a TV, radio, and a kitchen. She paid for her stay, planning to rest a while. In the morning, she wanted to call her friends and family.

Late that night, strange dreams took hold. She was at her house during the day. Strangers had filled the rooms, and women in large, old-fashioned dresses wandered about. One woman, wearing a pink dress, walked by Sandy's bedroom. She paused at the staircase, standing there, when an unrecognizable man came up behind her and pushed her.

"Watch out!" Sandy yelled, but the woman tumbled down the stairs, landing hard on her head.

The man who had pushed her was dressed in a hat, jacket, and gloves. He drew a pentagram on the wall, but it was upside down. As he ran away, the woman's body lay lifeless at the foot of the stairs.

"Samantha!" a man's voice cried out, and he rushed down the stairs to her. He cradled her, kissed her, and sobbed uncontrollably. Sandy assumed he was the woman's husband. He looked up, seeing the pentagram, and his crying intensified.

Sandy slowly made her way down the stairs. As she neared the lifeless woman, she gasped. The woman looked just like her. In fear, she jolted awake. Was it all just a dream? No, she was still at the cabin, and her husband was still wanted for murdering her cousin.

She began to like the old house, and she sensed that it, too, might have taken a liking to her. Maybe once Ralph was arrested, she could return to it. But then again, maybe not. She peeked out the window, only seeing wildlife moving through the night.

When her uncle was alive, she had visited him at her aunt's house. He enjoyed playing cards with her aunt Patty there, and often, he would sit and chat for hours. He owned more than one house, and the mansion was among them. Sandy had overheard her aunt mention he also had a lake house—not anything grand, just a simple retreat overlooking the water. Who would want to buy the mansion now, though?

Meanwhile, Ralph snuck back into the house after the police had left looking for him. He locked the door behind him, knowing his wife wasn't home—her car was gone. He sat down on the couch near the kitchen, lost in thought. The house felt deathly still, the shadows from the large grand staircase looming over him.

He turned around and noticed some old wallpaper behind him peeling off. Curious, he grabbed it and pulled. Underneath, he discovered light blue wallpaper, aged and brittle at the edges. He pulled again, revealing a faint line. Moving the couch, he peeled back more of the wallpaper until he uncovered something startling—a perfectly drawn upside-down pentagram.

He moved cautiously, wondering who had lived there before. He couldn't shake the feeling that this could have been the place where the woman had died. Sweat beaded on his forehead, and he unbuttoned his white-striped shirt, trying to cool off. His heart raced as he quickly ran up the stairs, his footsteps echoing down the hall.

But then, he saw it—Norman Jr.'s ghost. The sight made him freeze in terror. He turned and bolted back the other way, but in his panic, he slipped on the first two steps. The wooden staircase, thick and unforgiving, was no match for him. He tumbled, his body twisting as he rolled down, hitting his head with each agonizing bounce. By the time his head slammed against the floor, it was too late. He was dead.

The next morning, Sandy received the call she had been waiting for. Ralph was gone. She could finally return home to gather her things and start fresh. She decided to stay in the peaceful cabin for a few more days before looking for a new apartment in a nearby city.

She had no intention of selling the house. Two people had died there, and the place was aging faster than she was comfortable with. She collected her belongings—both old and new—and drove away, never looking back.

The Haunted Diary Page: Candles and Herbs

THE DREAMS CAME SWIFTLY that spring night. Sylvie found herself in a strange, sprawling, eerie house. It was gloomy, and she assumed she was ghost hunting for Rose. She was still hunting, but this time, not for extermination. Her stomach knotted with unease as faint sounds emerged from the third floor. At first, they were distant, subtle—until they grew into unmistakable footsteps.

As they drew closer, Sylvie, heart pounding, crept away. She didn't know this house, and she had no idea where to go. When the footsteps neared the stairs, she made a break for the front door. What was stalking her? Had a ghost followed her and her mother home?

Sylvie burst out the front door, running as fast as she could. Turning the corner, she recognized the familiar neighborhoods. But after one final glance at the house, she felt something ominous tailing her. The front door was swinging open and closed, as if moved by invisible hands.

Relieved to get home, she dashed into her room, slammed the door shut, locked it, and shoved a small dresser in front of it. Under the covers she crawled, trying to calm her racing heart. But when she opened her eyes again in the dream, someone was standing at the foot of her bed. A tall, shadowy figure, completely still.

She woke with a start, the sound of her little sister's voice downstairs mixing with the sizzle of breakfast being made. What a dream, she thought, shaking off the lingering unease. She reached under the mattress, grabbed her diary, and began to write. Was it a dream, or a warning?

My Dream Log

From now on, I'll record my dreams to track their frequency and any patterns. Maybe I can figure out if anyone is haunting our house. The Circle of Roses will always be there for me to lean on.

April

I was in a strange house. Something was chasing me. When I got home, I crawled into bed, but when I looked up, I saw it—at the foot of my bed! A shadow person. I woke up before it could do anything. I don't think it's worth calling Rose Cortez.

Sylvie went downstairs, trying to act casual. "Mom, did you hear anything strange last night?" She couldn't hide the nervousness in her voice. "Like... ghosts?"

"Actually, I did," Dana replied, her face clouded with unease. "There was this ticking noise, and then it turned into footsteps. Around midnight, I heard nails scratching at the downstairs window. Like a chalkboard." She mimed the noise with her fingers, claws out.

"Weird. I've been having strange dreams," Sylvie muttered, her diary still a secret. "Dana, do you have a diary?"

"No, but I want one," Dana said eagerly. "Maybe I'll start one in my notepad."

"I think there's a ghost after me," Sylvie admitted, her voice trembling. "I want to quit the Circle of Roses."

"I get it," Dana sighed. "We used to be rosebuds, but who wants to keep doing this anymore?"

"Exactly," Sylvie agreed, trying to steady her breath. "I'll keep an eye out for this ghost. I want to monitor my dreams more closely."

April

The next night, I had an even stranger dream. I woke up in my bed, the room dark. My journal sat on my desk. Suddenly, it flipped open to an empty page. As I watched, writing began to appear on its own. It said, Sylvie, I have been watching you. I know you and your sister don't like being in the roses. I want you to quit. Please do this so I don't have to force you.

I gasped and looked down at my feet. There he was again—the dark figure, the one I saw the night before. He just stared at me. Not like Star.

I lay back down, closing my eyes, and woke up. There he was, standing at the foot of my bed, right at my feet. I felt like I was going to explode, and before I could stop it, I screamed.

Dana and Mom came running in, their faces full of concern. "He was here!" I gasped. "I dreamed he wrote me a message in the diary, and when I woke up—he was right there!"

"Why? Who is he?" Dana asked, her voice shaking.

"I don't know. But we need to figure this out. It's not Star. I wonder if he's the one who sent this shadow ghost. It said that if I didn't quit, he would make me."

My family still doesn't know what to do, and I can't tell them about the deal I made. I pulled my diary out from under the mattress again and wrote, Who are you? I'm going to leave it out overnight to see if it answers. I'll tell Dana what I'm doing. For tonight, I'll stay in the guest room.

That night, sleep eluded Sylvie. A couple of times, after locking the door, she heard strange sounds in her room. She strained her ears for the sound of moving furniture but heard nothing. Maybe the ghost wouldn't reply, she thought. Maybe it only wanted to threaten her and haunt their home.

When morning arrived, the first thing Sylvie did was check her diary. There were no answers, just scribbles from a pen. I'm not quitting the roses. I won't have a job if I do. I'm not hurting anyone, she wrote.

"I'm not quitting," Sylvie told her mother. "I won't have a job if I do. I'm not hurting anyone."

"Okay," her mother replied. "But if anything starts bothering you, just come get me or your sister. I'm starting my job search today. I think I could do cashiering or receptionist work."

"So, you aren't going back to the Circle of Roses?" Sylvie asked.

"No. I don't think so," Lana answered.

"I'm not scared of the ghost anymore," Sylvie said. "But if it's alright, I'd like to stay in the guest room for a while."

"It's perfectly fine," her mother reassured her.

Dana, who had been quietly observing, piped up. "I wonder what the ghost will do. We'll have to get rid of it."

"There are many ways," Lana said, leading her daughters. "I'll think of one. It can't beat all of us together."

"I hope not," Sylvie said with a shudder. "I don't want to lose my job at the roses shop hunting ghosts."

"Mom, I had a bad dream last night," Sylvie began, looking serious. "When I woke up, my diary was open on my desk. I think it's a portal for ghosts. I don't want to get rid of it, though. I'll try hiding it under my mattress again, but the ghost might find it."

"Okay, give it a shot," Lana said, hanging laundry in the sunlit backyard.

"I'm not quitting my job," Sylvie continued. "I'm going to have a long talk with this ghost about that. I can even leave it a note. You know how I used to make jewelry?

"Yeah," her mother replied, glancing over her shoulder.

"I want to make jewelry again—bracelets with natural stones like amethysts and rose quartz—and sell them at the Circle of Roses shop," Sylvie said with determination.

"That's a great idea, Syl," Lana smiled. "I loved those bracelets you made last fall. You could even make them for ghost protection and store herbs inside or even incorporate them into the charm."

"That's exactly what I'm going to do," Sylvie replied, her eyes lighting up. "I'm going to get jewelry supplies today after I call Rose and ask if I can sell them at her shop. Then I'll write to the ghost in my diary. That should stop it. See you later, Mom!" She dashed for the door. "I'm going to make you a bracelet, one with herbs!"

"That's a great idea! We should all have one," Lana said, smiling warmly.

"That's right," Sylvie agreed. "We'll all get one, and I'll ask Dana what kind she wants." She waved to her mother and went inside to call Rose Cortez.

Shortly after, Sylvie burst into the room where Dana was. "Rose Cortez is going to let me sell my jewelry at her shop! I'm going to make bracelets for all of us with herbs that keep ghosts away." Dana jumped up, excited. "The herbs were Mom's idea!""

"That's so awesome!" Dana exclaimed. "I want to help."

"Okay! But you'll have to tell me how you want your bracelet made," Sylvie replied. Dana nodded in agreement. "I'm going to the store to get supplies—leather, chains, gemstones, beads, and herbs. I'll see you later, sis."

"See ya," Dana waved as she returned to eating her lunch on the couch.

Sylvie's desk was covered with jewelry kit supplies as she prepared to write a letter in her journal to the ghost. She needed to explain how she became a rose, how she makes jewelry, and how much she wanted to work at the Circle of Roses shop. She planned to write down the bracelet ideas after dinner.

Dana finished her spaghetti, and once she was done, Sylvie approached her. "Have you decided how you want your bracelet made?"

"I was thinking black leather with obsidian and fool's gold, with a couple of beads to match," Dana said, her eyes drifting to the ceiling as she imagined the design.

"That sounds perfect. And I know your wrist size, so I'll get started on yours tonight and finish it tomorrow." Sylvie paused for a moment, then added, "I have to wait and see what the ghost does about my note in the diary. If it doesn't work, I'll hide it." She gave Dana a grateful smile. "Thanks, Dane."

With that, Sylvie turned to her work.

"You won't believe this, Dana. I went to check my diary this morning and found this in it." Sylvie handed Dana a piece of paper. "A page from a diary stuffed right into mine, exactly where I wrote the note. It's a bunch of diary entries from someone who probably used to live here. It talks about an escalating haunting at different times of the day!"

Dana read it, her eyes widening as she sank into a chair. The entries were full of dread, and they went as follows:

'April. The grandfather clock in the hall chimed thirteen times tonight. Thirteen. It hasn't done that since... well, since before. Before the silence settled like a shroud over this house. Mom always said it was a bad omen when it misbehaved. I tried to wind it, but the key just spun, cold and slick in my hand.

The air in the attic is thick tonight, heavier than usual. It smells of dust and something else... something metallic, like old blood. I shouldn't go up there. I know I shouldn't. But the scratching started again. Faint at first, like a mouse behind the walls, but then it grew, insistent, right above my bedroom ceiling. It stops when I move, starts again when I'm still. It feels... deliberate. I wish we hadn't played with a Ouija board

I swear I saw a shadow in the corner of the living room earlier. Just a flicker, gone before I could focus. The cat hissed at it though. Whiskers flattened, back arched. He hasn't done that since... since him. The shadow-man that loomed over my bed.

The lullabies started again just after midnight. Faint, almost inaudible, like a child humming in the next room. But there are no children here. Just me. And the silence. And the scratching. And thirteen chimes.

I pulled the covers over my head, but the air under them is stale and smells faintly of lavender—Mom's perfume. It hasn't smelled of it in years.

Something just brushed my foot under the covers. The cat is downstairs.

I don't think I'm alone.'

"I wonder what it all means," Dana said, her voice low.

"I'm not sure. Maybe the ghost has decided to surrender. I didn't have any bad dreams last night. And that grandfather clock we have in the family room—it was left here by the last owners," Sylvie said, her voice trailing off. They hurried to the family room to see it.

The clock was tall and wooden, standing as high as Sylvie. Dana shook it, and it ticked loudly. Worn by time, it wasn't perfect. The time on it read nine a.m.

"That ghost who left this must be trying to scare you," Dana said, sounding skeptical.

"So now we have a haunted diary and a haunted grandfather clock," Sylvie muttered. "The diary page said it struck thirteen times."

"Weird. How do we get rid of both of them without Mom noticing?" Dana asked.

Sylvie lit two white candles with a lighter from the table. "We can't hide them, so I'll keep my diary in my room under the mattress. But I'll leave it out for now to see what happens next." A spark from one of the candles shot into the air.

Dana sat in a chair, flipping through the page. When she finished reading, she asked, "How do we know this isn't just a trick?"

"We don't," Sylvie admitted, "but we have a ghost to get rid of. I plan to use the herbs I was supposed to use at Star's house when I had to rid that evil spirit."

"Huh?" Dana had no idea what her sister was talking about. She ran her hand through her dark, medium-length hair.

"Don't tell anyone, but I had to get rid of an evil spirit that Rose Cortez thought was a ghost. I made a deal with it to leave it alone, so I took the herbs I was supposed to use and hid them. In return, I got lots of money from more ghost-hunting jobs. But that spirit was nasty—it blew me into the wall. When the realtor who wanted me to get rid of it insisted it was still around, I gave the job to Rose Cortez because the spirit threatened me. I'll use the herbs to keep the spirit away." Sylvie looked determined. "Let's go get those herbs I hid."

They drove out to the woodsy spot where Sylvie had hidden the herbs behind some trees, but to their dismay, they were gone. "Oh great. I hid them right here. We'll have to go get more."

The small plants weren't very expensive. When they returned home, they made a circle around the house with them.

As Dana placed the last plant, she said, "That ought to work," and they went inside to rest and eat.

When Sylvie saw her mother, Lana, coming home from a job interview, she noticed the plant circle around the house. She chuckled to herself. It took about ten angelica plants spaced out to completely encircle the house. She read the tags on the plants.

Upon entering the house, Lana asked, "Sylvie, why are there herbal plants around the house?"

"It's to try and get rid of the ghost. You know, I think that old grandfather clock might be something the ghost wants to haunt," Sylvie explained as she followed her mother into the kitchen.

"Okay, I understand. Besides, I like herbs. We can keep them in the backyard later. By the way, my interview went pretty well." Lana set her grocery bag on the counter. "I had to pick up a few things."

"That's great!" Sylvie said, eyeing the kitchen. "Can we order pizza tonight?"

"Sure, I don't mind," Lana said with a smile.

"I feel like pizza too. Tonight's going to be like a stakeout for ghosts," Sylvie said, her excitement building. "I have a feeling the herbs will work. If it does, I'll tell Rose Cortez. We made it like a protective circle." She hesitated. "Mom, this house was haunted before we moved in."

"How do you know that?" her mother asked, surprised.

"I just know. The haunted diary... it communicates things to me," Sylvie replied quietly.

"This had better stop tonight," her mother said firmly. "Or I'll take that diary away. You'd never see it again."

That night, Sylvie and Dana drank energy drinks as they finished the bracelets for the family. As Sylvie added beads to her mother's bracelet, the old grandfather clock struck. A gust of wind rustled outside. They counted the strikes: ten, eleven, twelve—and then, three seconds later, thirteen!

Sylvie stood up. A loud crash came from outside, and the wind grew stronger. Looking out the window, they saw the spirit! The plant circle was pulling the shadow-man into one of the pots, and several of the pots were knocked over, twitching but staying in place.

"Amazing!" Sylvie exclaimed.

"Yeah," Dana agreed, her voice full of awe.

The shadow-man let out a piercing yell, the unearthly sound echoing through the house. Then, as abruptly as it had started, he vanished into the dirt of the plant, and the wind stopped.

Lana ran into the room. "What was that?" she asked, clearly alarmed. "I heard someone yelling."

"It was the shadow-man," Sylvie said, a sense of calm settling over her. "But it looks like the plants got rid of him. It's okay now. Did you hear the wind?"

"Yes, it was nasty," her mom said.

"And the clock struck thirteen times," Dana added, her voice trembling slightly

"Okay, well, no more ghosts for the time being," Lana said, trying to sound reassuring. "I'm going to bed."

"I'm not," Sylvie replied, flopping down onto her bed with a dramatic sigh. Dana sank into a chair nearby. A moment later, Sylvie grabbed a nightlight from her room and plugged it into the wall of the guestroom she was staying in. They lay in silence, the steady ticking of the grandfather clock downstairs their only company as they drifted off to sleep.

Did you love *The Rose Cases: Sylvie's Diary*? Then you should read *The Haunted Rosebuds*[1] by Martha Wickham!

Lana is a psychic ghost hunter working in The Circle Of Roses shop. She wants to help solve a case when a man's wife leaves him because of ghosts tormenting her in the attic, but she ends up with a haunting dilemma of her own. Terra's ghost is haunting one of her teens in her small townhouse.Sylvie and Dana are teenagers who just want to live but when Sylvie's room is repeatedly thrashed, psychic Rose is called to investigate. She knows Terra from way back and thinks she wants more revenge, but why is the other teen Dana not affected? Sylvie and Dana have their own group called the Rosebuds. Started when they were kids, they wind up the only two in it. When old enough they will go into training to become real psychics. As for this story it is their first

1. https://books2read.com/u/bOpJ2g

2. https://books2read.com/u/bOpJ2g

everything, except their first time seeing a ghost. How long can Terra's ghost be kept a secret from Dana? And will Rose be able to solve both cases at once?

Read more at https://readmarthawickham.com/.

About the Author

Martha has studied writing with Writer's Digest and has an associate's degree. She has also written poems and songs and has even studied screen writing and horror at one time. She still practices writing and likes getting writing prompts, and her favorite author is VC Andrews. Listen to her hot new audiobooks at your favorite retailer.

Read more at https://readmarthawickham.com/.